Quartet  Qrime

DEATH OF A FANTASY LIFE

T. G. GILPIN

Death of a Fantasy Life

QUARTET QRIME

First published by Quartet Books Limited 1988
A member of the Namara Group
27/29 Goodge Street, London W1P 1FD

Copyright © 1988 T. G. Gilpin

British Library Cataloguing in Publication Data

Gilpin, T.G.
Death of a fantasy life.
I. Title
823′.914[F]   PR6057.I6/

ISBN 0-7043-2653-1

Typeset by Reprotype Limited, Peterborough, Cambs
Printed and bound in Great Britain at
The Camelot Press Ltd, Southampton

'By Jove!' said Flambeau; 'it's like being in fairyland.'
Father Brown sat bolt upright in the boat and crossed himself.

G. K. CHESTERTON, *The Sins of Prince Saradine*

For
ARLENE

One

The story really began one Friday evening in late August in Liz
Brennan's flat in the maze of streets squeezed between Shaftesbury Avenue and Oxford Street. Liz was holding open house for
her friends. She hadn't told them about the fifty pounds yet. She
was saving it.

She had spent the afternoon shopping for food and drink, and
most of the money had already gone. She preferred it that way.
She felt rather superstitious about having more money in her purse
than she needed. It was asking for trouble. When she had money –
and there had been times in her life when she had earned a lot –
she automatically adjusted her way of living so that what came in
matched what went out. She was never poor, but she never had
anything left over at the end of the month. The fifty pounds was a
windfall, to be spent as quickly and irresponsibly as it had come.

She had done her shopping in Old Compton Street, where
everyone knew her, and then sat in Soho Square for a while to
enjoy the sunshine before carrying her shopping bags back to the
flat. She no longer noticed whether people stared at her, but she
supposed they still did. She had never been able to look like a
respectable housewife, even for the short period that she had been
one, and it had stopped bothering her long ago.

It had been a beautiful day following a particularly awful one,
and everybody was out on the streets making the most of it.
London was a pleasure. It was a time for summer dresses and
shirtsleeves and lying on the grass in the park. Next day the
newspapers would talk about a heatwave. They would not talk
about Liz until the Monday morning, but then she would make
page one.

The general feeling in Fleet Street, even before Liz, was that it had been a pretty good year so far. There had been a royal divorce, Arabs were killing one another in Mayfair, Charlie Chaplin's body had been stolen, and smallpox had broken out in Birmingham. An unknown boxer with a silly name and no front teeth had beaten Muhammad Ali and the Cambridge boat had sunk at Barnes Bridge. An Englishwoman had sailed her yacht around the world, an Englishman was regarded as a good outsider for Pope, and Scotland had failed to win the World Cup.

On the political front, the former leader of the Liberal Party had been charged with conspiracy to murder, not to mention an abominable attitude towards dogs. Those who were never satisfied would have appreciated a decent sex scandal nearer to the government, but the prospect of an autumn election and the return of the Conservatives had raised hopes even in that quarter.

All in all, there was quiet satisfaction in the great houses of the fourth estate. And when a Soho stripper was found dead in her flat with her clothes removed and the swing which she used in her act tied round her neck, a number of editors, not normally the most devotional of men, were heard to profess a belief in the Almighty.

By evening a wind had blown up and there were a few drops of rain in the air, but it was still warm enough in the flat for Liz to leave the windows open to let some of the cigarette smoke out and the street noises in.

Outside the window, the day world of Soho was giving way to the night world. Lights had appeared over doorways that in the daytime had seemed to lead nowhere. The tourists and sightseers were being replaced by solitary men who knew what they wanted and where to find it. They zigzagged through the crowds on the pavements, looking down or straight ahead, and then veered suddenly to right or left and vanished from sight. The touts began to appear in the doorways of the strip clubs, murmuring their wares. The more established clubs relied on their displays of photographs, which were rarely changed. That generation of girls had left Soho years ago, gone and forgotten except from time to time when their bodies caught the light in the memories of men who had seen them.

The sex shops, bridging the day and night worlds, were closing and the last customers were being politely urged to make their final selection among the racks of magazines, searching for that certain elusive combination of face and breasts and clothes and camera-angle on which dreams could be built. The strip clubs would be open till midnight.

The flat was full of girls, strippers from the clubs where Liz worked. Some of them had taken the evening off and brought their boyfriends. Most of them just dropped in when they finished a spot at one of the clubs, ate something, drank something, chatted with friends, and disappeared again for their next spot. The boyfriends were tolerated, but expected to keep their mouths shut. There was a camaraderie among the women, even among enemies, which excluded the men.

The girls all seemed a little unreal. Make-up that was vivid enough for the garish light of the clubs looked clown-like in the smoky half-light of the flat. One girl with tired eyes and peeling make-up sat on the edge of Liz's table beside the plates of food, swinging her legs and laughing in long hysterical gasps. The soles of her feet were black – the badge of the girls who stripped barefoot, shuffling backwards and forwards on the dusty stage.

Towards midnight there were about a dozen of them left. They had eaten heaped, steaming plates of mince and spaghetti and drunk most of a crate of Spanish red wine. Everyone was fairly drunk and giggly, listening to Liz who was stretched out on the sofa, with her skirt up round her waist for comfort, chain-smoking and talking. She was a good talker and she smiled at everyone. Her face was deeply lined around the eyes and mouth, but they were lines of animation rather than age. She had probably been as wrinkled as a prune when she was eighteen. Her body was still good. Only Eric looked at her face, and Eric was crazy.

She had been at the clubs longer than anyone could remember, longer than any of the other girls, longer than the shifting and sinister population who owned them. Longer even than Monty. There were supposed to be a husband and children somewhere in her background, two husbands according to some versions, but she never spoke of them and no one asked. Liz was shop steward, counsellor and mother superior to half the strippers in London. If everyone who turned up that evening had come at the same time, they would have filled the little flat ten times over.

'Go on, Liz,' somebody said, 'tell us about the first time.'

'She can't remember,' Carla said. 'It's too bloody long ago.'

Carla was the black girl. She had brought her boyfriend Thomas

3

with her. Very big, very black, very sexy, and very much Carla's property, he was lying full length on the floor with his head against Carla's feet while she ruffled his hair with her toes. He had a huge bush of hair with a ballpoint pen stuck in it.

'Course she can remember,' he said. 'You're not that old, are you, Liz?'

Liz wasn't that old, though she was ten years older than anyone else in the room. She wasn't too old, which was what mattered. She knew plenty of strippers who wouldn't see forty again.

'I remember,' she said. 'It was in the back yard on a Saturday night and his name was John or Joe or something like that and it hurt like hell.'

'What a memory,' Carla said. 'I bet Eric can't remember either.' Eric grinned and clutched his drink. He was squashed up at the end of the sofa between Liz and Sylvia. Nobody had brought Eric. He just came. 'Cos it hasn't happened yet. Has it, Eric?' She paused for effect and said in her deep, throaty voice, 'You a virgin, Eric?'

'Leave him alone,' Sylvia said, and put a meaty arm round him. 'Eric's with me, aren't you, love?'

'That's not it,' Vicky said. There was silence and everybody stared at her. She lit another cigarette and stared back at them.

'Not what, honey?' Carla said, and giggled.

'Nothing,' Vicky said. 'Forget it.'

Vicky was there because Liz had invited her. None of the other girls would have done. Vicky was different. She had three A-levels and nobody was allowed to forget it. She was also the youngest and the prettiest. When she wasn't in a state of black depression and refusing to speak to anyone, she had the sharpest tongue in the business. On a good day she could even get the better of Carla who was equally poisonous but less intelligent. Carla would then take it out on Sylvia who was less intelligent than everybody.

'What isn't it, honey?' Carla sensed that Vicky was having one of her rare vulnerable days and was determined to make the most of it. She moved her foot down inside the open neck of Thomas's shirt, and waited.

Vicky stubbed out the cigarette she had just lit and finished her wine. She was a woman born out of her time. A Romantic would have seen her as the vampire, pale and phthisic, leading men to hell. The opinion of most of the regulars at the clubs was that her breasts were too small. Her hair was very black, cut short like a

4

boy's, and her skin very white. She had dark shadows under her eyes, and her fingers were unnaturally long. Men stopped and stared at her, though for her strangeness rather than her beauty.

'It's not the pain,' she said. 'OK, it hurts the first time. But it's not the pain.'

'What is it, honey?'

Vicky looked at Carla and then at the others in the room.

'Forget it,' she said.

'You really hate them, don't you, honey?'

Vicky said nothing. There was a long silence while everyone waited to see what else was coming. Nothing else was coming. The conversation picked up again, slowly and quietly. Thomas shuffled around on the floor.

'In my opinion,' Liz said, 'there are two things you need to be a stripper.'

Thomas made a suggestion, as she knew he would, and everyone howled at him. Carla dug her toenails into his neck and he squealed and grabbed her foot.

'No, children,' Liz said, 'not what you might think.'

'Tell us, honey.'

'Well, first of all, you've got to like men. I don't mean you have to like all of them. But you've got to like some men.' She looked at Vicky. 'Well I have to. Otherwise I couldn't do it. Second, you've got to be a bit of an actress. You've got to lay it on a bit. They don't just want to look at you standing there with nothing on. They might as well be looking at a corpse on a slab. They want to feel there's something going on between you and them. It doesn't matter what it is. You can pretend you're a raving nympho and you can't wait for them all to get their hands on you. That goes over quite well.'

Somebody giggled and said, 'Oh yeah'.

'Then again,' she said, 'you can do it the other way. Snarl at them, insult them, give them a hard time, let them think you hate them. You hate undressing in front of them but you've got to do it anyway. They like that too. It's the old master and slave thing. Makes them feel powerful. That's the way I do it.'

She paused. 'The older you get,' she said, and everyone went silent, 'the older you get, the more of an actress you've got to be. They don't want to look at old flesh unless there's something going on. You've got to make up for being old. So I give them a hard time.'

'They love it, honey,' Carla said.

'Yeah, I know.'

'But you don't really hate them?' Sylvia said. She was upset by all this talk about hate. She didn't understand everything that had been said, but she sensed that it went against her philosophy of life which was, briefly, that we're all here to have as much fun as we can, preferably without hurting anyone else.

'No, love,' Liz said, 'I don't hate them. Not really. It's all a bloody game.' Then she suddenly remembered what the party was all about and what she'd been meaning to tell them. 'Hey,' she said, 'where do you think the money came from for all this booze, then?'

'Rich Arab,' Carla said.

'No. Bloke with a hole in his pocket.'

'You mean somebody dropped it?'

'Not quite. Vicky knows all about this. Do you want to tell them, Vicky, or shall I?'

Vicky did not want to tell them.

'OK,' Liz said, 'here goes. Bloke comes into Monty's. Pays his money, gets his ticket, goes in to watch the show. I was on my way out. Vicky was with me, weren't you, Vicky? Anyway, he drops this bit of paper. Actually it was a card, you know, like a business card, with his name and address and some other stuff on it. Well, we were going to leave it at the desk for him to pick up on his way out. Then we decided to have a bit of fun with it. He was a smart-looking bloke, fifties, nice suit, the sort who'd have a wife somewhere who wouldn't exactly approve. So we wrote a letter, me and Vicky, and sent it off to the address on the card. Dear Sir, you have been observed frequenting certain premises in St Anne's Court commonly known as a strip club. If you do not want this fact advertised, kindly enclose fifty pounds in used fivers and send to the above address. Thanking you in advance. Your obedient servants, Elsie and Doris.'

'You don't mean he sent it,' Carla said.

'He bloody did. Fifty quid in used fivers. Turned up a few days later. We only meant it as a joke. You know, give him a few sleepless nights. We never expected him to send it. We'd never have done anything if he hadn't. It was just a joke. Anyway, he paid up. So here we are.'

'You should send it back,' Sylvia said.

'Don't be daft, love. He can afford it. Have another drink,

courtesy of Mr X.'

'You wouldn't feel like giving us his name, honey?'

'No, love,' Liz said. 'I wouldn't.'

After midnight, when the clubs had closed, a number of girls dropped by who hadn't been able to get away during the evening. They came in in a bunch, dripping wet, with one umbrella between them, holding plastic bags and newspapers over their heads. Liz looked out of the window. The lights were still on in some of the clubs and their reflections drowned in the wet pavements. A passing car searched out an opening with its headlights in the bead curtain of rain and entered cautiously.

Liz lit the gas fire, the party got its second wind, she told her Mr X story again, and they carried on until two in the morning when she finally threw them out.

When they were leaving, Vicky discovered that the key to her flat was missing from her handbag.

'Give it back, Thomas,' somebody said.

Liz tried to persuade her that she'd lost it and it would turn up, and gave her the duplicate which she kept at her place in case of emergencies. Vicky was not convinced.

'One of you's got it,' she said.

When she had finally seen everybody off, Liz poured herself a last drink and sat with her feet up. She decided she would tackle the washing up in the morning.

She died the following night, a little less than twenty-four hours later. She never went to bed much before two when she was working. She was thinking about getting ready when there was a knock at the door. She thought one of her friends had come round to see her. They often came late. The girls who lived near the clubs were always in and out of each other's flats, especially those who were between boyfriends. Liz, by choice, had been between for almost a year and was seriously considering staying that way.

She opened the door, gave her visitor an unenthusiastic smile, and died instantly from a blow to the head as she turned back into the room. He had hit her with a large glass ashtray from the table by the door.

When she was dead and her clothes were removed and the swing

7

placed in position, her killer stood and looked at her for a few moments. It did not seem enough. She had died too easily. He had come not just to kill her, but to wipe her out of his mind. He began systematically smashing everything in the little flat that was capable of being smashed. Pictures, cups, plates, glasses, everything was broken. He picked up the ashtray and smashed it. Finally, the light was switched off and the door was closed.

Two

It was Sylvia. Eric was disappointed.

'And now ... gentlemen ...' said the bored voice from behind the curtain, which he recognized as Monty's, 'the very beautiful ... Sylvia.'

Sylvia bounced on, grinning all over her face, cheerful as ever. Eric hated her for that. She spotted him. A cheery smile for Eric. A cheery smile for that decrepit old git installed in his usual seat in the front row and scrabbling in his pocket for his bag of sweets.

'Christ,' Sylvia said, 'you here again.' She said this every time she saw him, which must be just about every day, and he would give her a ghastly smile and offer her a sweet. She took it, said thank you and popped it in her mouth. Eric felt sick.

Sylvia got on with it. It wasn't very good. It never was with Sylvia, though it went over big with the over-eighties. Never mind. Vicky would be on soon. Vicky was the best thing they'd had since the woman on the swing. But she was dead.

Fifteen minutes later, Sylvia needed a gin and tonic. Unusually, she had a clear forty-five minutes before she was due on for her next spot at the Reveille which was five minutes' walk away, round the corner in Frith Street.

She came out of the dressing room at the side of the stage. There were half a dozen men lined up in the aisle waiting for an empty seat. A lot of the girls hated this bit, said it was worse than the stripping. Sylvia rather enjoyed it. Most of the clubs now had a back door so the girls could get out when their spot was over without going past the audience. Monty's, of course, did not. Everything on the cheap. She didn't know what all the fuss was

9

about, anyway.

Men were funny. When the girls were up on the stage with nothing on, they'd be all agog, twisting their heads round to get a better view of every inch. But when you came out of the dressing room and walked right past them, they all looked the other way or sat reading their newspapers. She would sometimes stop halfway up the aisle and stare at them. Frightened them to death.

When the aisle was crowded, most of the girls just put their heads down and barged through. This was not Sylvia's way.

'Excuse me,' she said, very politely, looking the nearest one straight between the eyes.

They plastered themselves against the wall and she swept through. Occasionally, one of them, one of the younger ones, would look her up and down. Then she'd give him a good look up and down and that would be the end of that.

Nobody ever touched her. Not that it would have done them any good. She was five foot six, a little under thirteen stone, and well able to look after herself.

Mr Smith was on his way out of the door.

'Hello, Mr Smith,' she said, 'had enough for one day?'

He started fishing in his pocket. Oh God, he was going to offer her another sweet. They were horrible sticky lemon things and she had not managed to spit today's out behind the curtain as she usually did. She could still taste it. Most of the girls refused them, but she hadn't the heart. He was a harmless old sod.

'No thanks, Mr Smith,' she said. 'Wouldn't want me to get fat now, would you?'

This brought on a fit of convulsions, and she was quite worried about him for a minute. He managed to pull himself together, pocketed his bag of sweets and tottered out. Sylvia always made jokes about her size before other people did. She was not as insensitive about it as she seemed. She had been on a diet for months, but her heart wasn't in it.

The pub was nearly empty. It was the local for people from the clubs. There were a couple of girls she knew vaguely, and she gave them a wave before perching herself on one of the stools at the bar. It was a nice pub. She avoided the tourist traps in Leicester Square. A waitress in one of them had once lectured her on the old English custom of tipping in pubs and Sylvia had been on the point of physical violence when she was asked to leave.

She was halfway through her gin and tonic when she noticed the old boy in the corner, peering at her over the top of a half of bitter, showing her a set of extremely bad teeth, and talking to himself. She had seen him at Monty's at the beginning of her spot, in the second row, and now he was in the pub looking her up and down and muttering to himself.

Now Sylvia held very strict views about this. When she was in the clubs, any man who paid the price was entitled to look at her as much as he liked. That was her job. She did not resent it, as some of the girls did, or make it obvious that she despised them, which she didn't anyway. They got what they paid for. But once she was outside the clubs, it was different. Occasionally a man would follow her out of a club, staring at her. They never tried anything, just stared. Some of the girls got rather neurotic about it and were convinced that any man who looked at them in the street must have seen them in a club. They said it made them feel dirty. That, in Sylvia's opinion, was nonsense. She had never felt dirty, but she didn't like it and she had her own way of dealing with it.

She picked up her drink and went over to where he was sitting. He was staring right at her and still talking to himself. She put her drink down on his table, rested a large, red-nailed hand beside it and placed the other hand on her hip. It was her intimidating pose. Never failed. The table wobbled slightly.

'Excuse me,' she said, 'do you mind?'

The man blinked and seemed to see her for the first time. He stood up and held out his hand.

'Ponton,' he said.

Sylvia ignored this.

'Look love,' she said, 'you're not at the club now. You've had your money's worth. So drink your beer and forget it.'

'You appear to be under a misapprehension,' the man said, and blinked at her again.

It began to dawn on Sylvia that she was making a horrible mistake. When she looked at him close up, she was quite sure he was not the man from the second row. She had never seen him before. She felt awful. He was still standing up with his hand stuck out. She shook it and sat down. He sat down.

'I'm terribly sorry,' she said. 'I thought I saw you in the ... I thought you were staring at me ... I mean ...'

He smiled at her. God, his teeth were awful. Long and yellow with no gums. Sylvia put him at about fifty. A friendly enough sort of face, a bit too red. Not healthy red. Blotchy. Brown suit, the

11

sort her father wore when he was dressed up. Made to last twenty years and well on the way. Grey pullover with the tie tucked inside. Hankie stuck up his shirt cuff. All he needs is the pipe.

The man took out a pipe and clamped it between his teeth. They might not be beautiful but they were strong. He looked as if he could chomp through an oak door.

'I may have been staring at you, or in your direction rather. It wasn't intentional. I'm sorry if I annoyed you. I was rather engrossed.'

'You were talking to yourself,' she said.

'I'm afraid I appear to do that.' He smiled, took out a box of Swan Vestas and got his pipe going. 'I was thinking about vowel systems, actually. I may have been practising some of the sounds to myself. Occupational hazard really. People do tend to think you're mad.'

Sylvia took this with equanimity. She had got used to people saying things to her which she didn't understand. She found it best to be non-committal.

'Oh yes,' she said.

He seemed to find this amusing.

'Permit me,' he said. He took out a wallet and handed her a small white card. In the centre, in heavy black print, it said,

Anthony Ponton MA
Reader in the Department
of Linguistics in the
University of Southampton

There was a phone number in the bottom corner. Nobody had ever given her their card before. She gave it back, holding it carefully by one corner.

'Pleased to meet you,' she said.

Vicky was on, doing her act with the hammock, and Eric felt better. Monty had introduced her in his bored, disembodied voice, 'Gentlemen ... the very lovely ... Vicky.' The curtains opened and there she was, with that look on her face that made his hands sweat and his heart stop.

There are three kinds of strippers. There are the cows like Sylvia who smile at everybody and try to look as if they're enjoying themselves. There are the ones who look bored sick, stare at a point somewhere on the back wall and do their act without ever

12

looking at the audience. And then there are the ones like Vicky, who look at the men with total contempt, real hatred. It mattered terribly to Eric to know that Vicky hated him. It was a real contact, like love. Only better, stronger.

He never took his eyes off her face. He knew she couldn't stand that. The men could gape at her body until they were sick and she just despised them. But if somebody stared at her face and never looked down, it really rattled her. He had tried this with the other girls and it generally worked, but it was best with Vicky. She tried everything she knew to get him to look at her body, but he just kept staring at her face and smiling until she turned all her hatred on him and him alone, and her eyes burned with it.

There was no one like Vicky, had been no one since the woman with the swing.

Sylvia was on her second gin and tonic. Ponton was still nursing his half but the pipe had been refilled and he was puffing away happily. She had taken quite a fancy to the old boy, in a nice sort of way. Sylvia had, after some hesitation, admitted to her profession.

'A striptease artist,' he said. 'Really?' He sounded quite impressed. He said he had never seen a striptease. It might even have been true.

She had got on to the subject of Liz's murder of which she had, after all, been almost a witness. He had never heard of it, though it had been in all the papers for weeks. Front page. Photos of Liz in her costume. Out of her costume. Photos of the swing. Even on one occasion, and probably by mistake, a photo of Sylvia.

She suddenly remembered the time and looked at her watch. She was late for her spot at the Reveille. That would mean a fine deducted from her pay. Bugger it, she thought.

'Anyway,' she said, 'Liz had this act with a swing. Just a bit of wood and two ropes. It was hooked up on a bar above the stage. She used to swing on it and strip off.'

'Tricky,' Ponton said.

'Not too bad. Anyway, when she'd got everything off, she sat on the swing, stuck her legs out and swung into the audience. Not too far. By the time they realized she was coming, she was on her way back. Then she turned round, facing away from them like, with her bum stuck over the edge of the seat and swung out backwards. It was very popular.'

13

'I can imagine.'

'She was a real sod, Liz. Used to insult them all the time. You dirty old buggers. You're all pathetic. That sort of thing. No reaction. There never is. They just look at you. Like talking to a lot of fish. Anyway, she lived just round the corner. She was a neighbour of mine. A lot of the girls live round here for convenience. The others live as far away as they can. I used to drop in and see her a lot. She was dead funny, Liz. Make a pig laugh.'

Sylvia stopped and took a deep swig of her gin and tonic. She realized she was close to tears. She'd talked about it often enough before, but it always caught her that way. She'd been fond of Liz. There were some of the others she wouldn't have minded seeing off. She snuffled.

Ponton fetched a huge handkerchief out of his shirt cuff and offered it.

'Thanks,' she said, and blew her nose loudly. 'Where was I? About a month ago it was. Saturday. We'd all been round to her place for a party the night before. Anyway, she was about to go on when she sees one of the ropes on the swing is frayed. I saw it. Looked as if it'd go any minute. Right, she says, I'm not going on with that and land in the middle of those buggers. Don't know what might happen to me, she says. Nobody had another rope, so she went off home and took the swing with her. Said she'd get it fixed in the morning. Well, I was on at Monty's all evening and I didn't get off until about midnight. I didn't have a spot until the afternoon the next day and I didn't feel like going to bed. I ended up going round to Liz's. I knew she'd be up. She went to bed about two in the morning and got up in time for the first spot at twelve. So I went round to see her. Just for a chat and a drink and a bit of a laugh, you know. We used to sit up all night sometimes.' Sylvia paused and blew her nose again. 'So I was the one who found her. I knew something was wrong when she didn't answer the door. So I let myself in. I had a spare key.'

'How awful,' Ponton said, declining the return of his handkerchief.

'She had the swing wrapped round her neck. Well, one end of the rope round her neck and the rest of it on the floor. I thought she'd been strangled, but the police said she was dead before the rope was put round her. Hit on the back of the head. All her clothes had been pulled off.'

'Was she assaulted? Sexually, I mean.'

14

'No, that's the funny part. He'd never touched her, not that way. He must have pulled her clothes off, then just stood there looking at her.'

Sylvia broke down completely. Huge tears squeezed out of her eyes and ran down her cheeks. Her make-up made black streaks down her face.

'Sorry,' she said. 'It was just so horrible. Like a bomb had gone off. Everything smashed. He even tore up her photos. And Liz just lying there in the middle of it all.'

'I don't really know what I'm doing up here,' Ponton said. 'Rather a quandary really.'

'Oh yes.' Sylvia pulled herself together a bit. She got the little mirror out of her handbag and did her make-up.

'I'm supposed to be looking for my nephew. Would you like another?' He pointed at Sylvia's empty glass.

'No thanks. I think I've had enough.' She gave him one of her best smiles to show she was all right. He'd seemed quite concerned about her. She knew why he'd changed the subject and she was grateful.

'I was his legal guardian, you see. Rather an empty title, but there it is. Not any more of course. He's well over age now.'

Sylvia wiped her nose on Ponton's handkerchief and tried to pay attention. He had got another pipe going. Sylvia had stopped smoking, though she wondered if she ought to start again in the interests of her diet. She could murder a fag right now.

'Go on,' she said.

'He was sixteen when his mother died. She was my sister. His father had died when he was a baby. We all rallied round of course, but she insisted on bringing him up on her own. Very creditable really, I suppose. I never got on with him terribly well, and by the age of sixteen he neither needed nor wanted an old bachelor like me for a guardian. Still, there you are. I feel responsible.'

'Where is he now?'

'Well ... I'm not boring you with the family history, am I?'

'Course not.' Sylvia glanced down at her watch. She was about to miss her second spot. Oh well, she thought, a day's a day.

'He's up here somewhere. London. His mother left him quite a bit of money, you see. A few months ago he drew the lot and disappeared. We've had a postcard but it didn't say much. I don't know if he's working or what he's doing.' He showed her his teeth, pipe clenched in them. She wished he wouldn't. She quite liked him with his mouth shut. 'Well, the family, what's left of it, are getting rather agitated and so I was dispatched, as it were, to come up and do something about him. So here I am. In search of Eric.'

'Eric?' she said. 'Hang about. What's his other name? What's he look like?'

'Eric Wells. Oh, fairly tall, thin, blond hair.'

'Christ,' she said, 'Eric. Everybody knows Eric. He's a regular. He was in Monty's half an hour ago. He's got a flat in Dean Street. Does the clubs every day. All the girls know him.'

'Good heavens.' Ponton was staring at her. He had actually taken his pipe out of his mouth. 'But what's he doing, apart from going to clubs?'

'Nothing.' Ponton still looked blank. 'Look,' she said, 'we get them sometimes. Hangers on. They do the clubs, chat the girls up, get to know our names, sit in the front row and talk to us when we're doing a spot. I don't know why. They must get something out of it. They're a bit pathetic usually.'

'And Eric does that?'

'That's right. He's been around for months. We're all used to him now. They don't usually last that long.'

'I see.' Ponton put his pipe back in his mouth and took a long time to get it going. 'And you have his address?'

'Oh yes.' Sylvia told him the address. He fetched a little black book and a pencil out of his pocket and wrote it down.

'Well, I really am most grateful to you. It's a wonderful coincidence really. Is there anything else you can tell me about him?'

'He's got a crush on Vicky. Follows her round. Turns up wherever she's got a spot. Drives her round the twist.'

'Vicky?'

'One of the strippers,' Sylvia said. 'Talks a lot of rubbish. I mean if you're going to strip you've got to take care of yourself. You've got to look nice. It's part of the job. She looks like something the cat brought in. Says it's politics. How can looking scruffy be politics? Says she doesn't shave her armpits for political reasons. What's that got to do with politics, being hairy?'

'Ah,' he said, fussing about with his pipe again and giving himself a crooked little smile, 'that's an interesting statement. Do

16

you mean that she doesn't shave and her reason for not shaving is political, or do you mean that she shaves but for reasons which are not political? The sentence is ambiguous, you know. Depends on the intonation.'

'Come again.'

Ponton said it again slowly and then said the sentence two different ways, with his voice going up and down in different places, wagging his finger in the air like somebody conducting a band.

Sylvia still didn't get it. Ponton tried again. She thought about it for a while, then her face lit up.

'Y'bugger,' she said affectionately, and punched Ponton playfully on the shoulder. He winced.

'You were talking about Vicky,' he said, easing his arm up and resting it on the table.

'She's got an act with a hammock. See-through. Like a fishnet. Quite good. I thought of copying it but I couldn't get one strong enough.'

'Do you think you could introduce me?'

'To Vicky?'

'Yes. I think it might be helpful. If it's no trouble. She's not a friend of yours, I gather?'

'Can't stand her,' Sylvia said, 'but I'll introduce you. It's no good being sensitive, though. She's not very nice.'

'Oh that's all right,' he said. 'I know lots of people who aren't very nice.' And he showed her his teeth again.

As they left the table, Ponton was fiddling with one of the beer mats. He'd been playing with things on the table all the time they'd been talking, but she hadn't paid much attention to him. Now she saw what he was up to. He had four beer mats evenly spaced around the middle of the table. His glass was in the middle of one, Sylvia's glass in the middle of another, the ashtray in the middle of the third, and his tobacco and matches in the middle of the fourth. Not roughly in the middle. Exactly in the middle. And his box of matches was exactly in the middle of the tobacco tin. If Sylvia moved something, he'd moved it back.

He picked up his tobacco and matches and slipped them into his pocket. Somebody had told her something once about men who were always tidying things but she couldn't remember what it was. She wondered if he knew he was doing it.

17

Eric left the club after Vicky's spot. He couldn't watch the others. His brain was too full of her. She had been wonderful. He had forced her, forced her by the sheer power of his will to turn all her contempt, her hatred on him. She had done things with her body that she had never done before. He knew what she was doing, but he had never for one instant taken his eyes off her face. And he had been repaid. Better than ever. It was all too much. He hoped to God that Vicky was not going to die, but he was afraid for her.

Three

A visiting American professor had once remarked to Ponton that there was something peculiarly decadent about the English, watching striptease at noon. This was the occupation in which Ponton found himself engaged the following morning.

After leaving the pub, he had walked up Tottenham Court Road and spent the afternoon in Dillon's looking at the new linguistics books. Foyle's was closer of course, but he still liked to maintain certain standards. Sylvia had walked with him part of the way and lectured him on what he was going to do about Eric. He then took a tube to Archway and walked into Highgate where he was staying. Actually, the house was rather closer to Archway than to Highgate proper, but his hosts had made it very clear that they lived in Highgate and not in Archway and Ponton took their word for it.

He had taken over the bottom floor of a large three-storey house which belonged to a couple he had known for years. They lived in the top two floors and normally rented the other one out to students, but Ponton had managed to get the use of it for a week or so while they were between tenants. His rooms were below street level at the front but at garden level at the back, and he could sit in his living room during the day with the French windows open on to the garden and forget that he was in London at all. The situation was ideal. If he wanted company he could go upstairs and spend an evening with friends. If he wanted to be alone, he could stay in his own rooms. On that evening he stayed downstairs, thinking about Eric and his encounter with Sylvia.

He was still rather bemused by the experience. By the time they had parted she was talking to him as if he were an old friend, or possibly a fellow striptease dancer. He found this disconcerting. They had got into conversation through some silly mistake on her part and before he knew where he was they were discussing some gruesome murder which he was expected to know all about and she was about to burst into tears. Ponton had promptly changed the subject to Eric, who had been nagging at the back of his mind all day, and it transpired that Sylvia knew a great deal about him. From then on their friendship was cemented, as it were, and he still couldn't understand quite how it had happened.

Sylvia was surprisingly easy to talk to, and Ponton did not normally find women easy to talk to. He had always been very aware, perhaps inhibitingly aware, of the niceties of social interaction. It was another occupational hazard, like making funny noises to oneself. He was hopelessly clumsy at putting these rules into practice, but he knew how one was supposed to behave. Sylvia had no idea. She was both enormously sociable and totally unsocialized. She had no concept of social distance. Ponton had crossed the gulf from stranger to intimate in a matter of minutes simply because she had no idea that the gulf existed. He found this disconcerting but at the same time rather refreshing.

At quite which point in their relationship she had arranged that he would visit a striptease club the next morning and then meet her for lunch he was not sure. But she had arranged it and, amazingly, he seemed to have agreed. She had admittedly given him very sound advice about Eric, and perhaps he had fallen into the habit of agreeing with everything she said.

First of all, she had suggested that if Eric wanted to spend his time and his money living the bohemian life in Soho, why not leave him alone and let him get on with it? Young men needed to sow their wild oats. No doubt Ponton had sown his at some time, had he not? The answer to this was actually no, but Ponton did not say so. His own adolescence had been spent discovering a quite different world, far more mysterious and exciting, the world which lay hidden in books. He did not feel that Sylvia would be sympathetic to such a confession. Secondly, she said, if family pressure were such that he was obliged to do something about Eric, then he should make some effort to understand the boy's way of life. It would at least give them something to talk about. Besides, Ponton deserved a treat. He had never seen a striptease, which struck Sylvia as nothing less than disgraceful, and he would enjoy himself.

She was, of course, absolutely right, though perhaps not about the treat. Sooner or later he would have to talk to Eric and the task would be easier if he had some insight into the way of life which Eric had made his own. Ponton had always avoided talking to his nephew. He still remembered him as a truly nauseating little boy and he had no rapport with little boys, never as far as he could remember having been one himself. Ponton was one of those people who are born middle-aged. But Sylvia could be remarkably persuasive. He got up in the morning absolutely dreading it, but he duly presented himself at ten minutes to noon at the door of the Snow White (proprietor Monty Snow) in St Anne's Court.

'Good morning, sir. You a member?'

'No. I am a friend of Miss Mothersill.' Ponton had enquired Sylvia's surname, assuming that some kind of recommendation would be necessary.

'Two pounds, sir, and a pound for membership.'

The man gave Ponton a card to fill in. The card informed him that his membership would not become valid until twenty-four hours had elapsed from the time of his signing the card.

'Do I understand that I must come back tomorrow?'

'Just fill in the card, sir. Show's on now.' The man waved his arm to indicate a curtain and a wail of pop music from within.

Ponton wrote his name. He came to the space for his address.

'Which address would you prefer? I'm normally resident in Southampton but I do have a temporary address in London if that would be more ...'

'Put any address you like, sir,' the man said.

Ponton handed back the card. The man glanced at it, looked up quizzically as if he were about to ask whether his customer could not come up with a more plausible name than Ponton, took the three pounds, gave Ponton a ticket stub and waved his arm towards the curtain.

'Show's on now, sir.'

The show, as it happened, was not. Ponton had time to find a seat and spend a few minutes examining his surroundings and his fellow spectators. He was standing in the aisle which ran down one side of the room, at the end of which was a curtained stage. The rest of the room was occupied by seven or eight rows of cinema seats. Ponton chose a seat at the end of the fourth row, next to the aisle, and looked around. The lights kept changing colour. It was like being trapped inside a traffic light.

There were about a dozen men already there, more than he would have expected at lunch-time on a weekday and considering the number of clubs there were to choose from. Most of them were old, older than Ponton. He gathered that several of them had regular seats. Some of the seats in the front row which had been empty when he arrived were quickly occupied by elderly gentlemen who made straight for them and settled down, nodding briefly to their neighbours and stowing overcoats and parcels under the seats. Most men read newspapers. The *Express* and the *Mail* were popular, with the occasional *Mirror* and *Sun*. There was one *Financial Times*. A thesis topic for one of his students suggested itself to Ponton, but he rejected it on grounds of propriety.

The pop music, which had been playing continuously since he came in, stopped. Someone carefully folded a newspaper and slipped it down the side of the seat. A voice crackled through a microphone somewhere at the side of the stage, wished them good afternoon and announced the beginning of the show. The pop music began again.

There was a noise of somebody clambering on to the stage and apparently falling over. A female voice was heard uttering an expletive. The music changed to something slower and, one presumed, more seductive. The curtains opened to reveal a girl standing with her back to the audience. She was rubbing her knee.

Ponton stayed for an hour and then left. He felt that he had seen enough striptease for one day, if not for a lifetime. The man at the door wished him a cheery good afternoon.

It was, of course, ridiculous and awful. Grotesque. Ponton had always had a very vivid awareness of the absurdity of sex. People sticking bits of themselves into other people was not a serious activity. For this reason he hated most modern novels. He could not read love poetry, even very good love poetry. He could just about tolerate the Come-and-kiss-me-sweet-and-twenty stuff that was simply designed to get the girl into bed and treated sex as a transitory physical satisfaction like eating, but he hated John Donne.

He did not regard himself as a prude. He was, given his age and his background, unusually tolerant of the sexual habits of others. He did not find it reprehensible or immoral. He simply found it ridiculous. This was no doubt the reason he had never been any good at it, and he had given up the attempt at an early age. He had been much happier since.

He tried to consider the performance he had just witnessed in an objective way. It was as banal as a church social. He was, for example, surprised by the sedate atmosphere, almost an air of senility, which pervaded the whole proceedings. To be frank, he had expected a crowd of youngish louts, or at least middle-aged louts, bawling their appreciation at the spectacle of women undressing. Far from it. The audience had been old, apparently respectable, and probably incapable of bawling at anybody. They sat politely through each act and read their newspapers in the interval. They conducted themselves with admirable decorum. A university staffroom was a riot by comparison. Apart from the fact of women poking their private parts under people's noses, it could have been recommended as a Sunday outing for the family. What on earth was going on?

The attitude of the girls themselves was interesting. One had bounced on holding a teddy bear with which she proceeded to conduct an unlikely relationship. Another had worn a school uniform and sucked her thumb. It was these acts which had been greeted with the greatest appreciation. The dancers who were mature women and who had not pretended to be otherwise had been received with indifference, whereas the sight of some creature armed with a teddy bear and a lollipop and her hair done up in floppy ribbons had brought the audience as close to any sign of animation as they were capable.

It was all incredibly undignified in elderly gentlemen. He wondered if any of his colleagues entertained themselves in this way on their trips to London. He hoped not. He could not help thinking he had made the right decision all those years ago.

There were, however, two things which troubled him. The first was Sylvia. He had been careful to ascertain from her the times when she would be performing, and had gone at a different time. He could not have watched it. Ponton liked Sylvia. Intellectually, of course, she was not at the level of his weakest student – or even his weakest colleague – but he liked her and it troubled him that she was a part of what he had just seen, and an enthusiastic part at that. She had given him the impression that she enjoyed her work. He preferred not to think of her in that way.

The other matter was a nagging at the back of his mind. He had tried looking at the striptease as an interesting social phenomenon, as a horrible example of what could happen to elderly men, and as a particularly ludicrous example of human beings conducting their

23

sexual business. But there was something else. What was going on in the heads of those dreadful old men? He thought of Liz Brennan on her swing, and then with the swing around her neck, and it frightened him.

He had not, thank God, seen Eric. He had never been able to talk to the wretched boy and he felt even less able to do so now.

Ponton was almost at the corner of Oxford Street when he was accosted by a large person in tweeds. He had already been interrupted once in his hurried progress from the vicinity of the club by a very smart young lady who had offered him her services, which he had declined. This second lady did not appear to be in the same profession. She was Ponton's age or rather more, stout with a red face, and would have looked more at home supervising a gymkhana in the New Forest than bothering passers-by on the edges of Soho.

'Excuse me,' she said, 'you may be interested in this,' in a tone of voice which suggested that it would be a severe abrogation of Ponton's moral duty to be other than interested.

He looked briefly at the card which had been placed in his hand. It was about the size of a postcard and bore at the top, in heavy black print, the letters

SSS

Ponton experienced a moment of utterly absurd terror in which he imagined that he had been observed leaving the club, followed, and was now being arrested by some kind of secret police. He read on. The next line calmed his fears somewhat.

THE SAVE SOHO SOCIETY

He looked at the lady in tweeds and smiled.

'Have you read it?' she said.

'Not yet.'

'Please do so.'

Ponton read. The card informed him that the district of London commonly known as Soho, supposedly named after a hunting cry, was a unique part of Britain's heritage. Long associated with the artist and the craftsman, and possessing a distinctive European flavour, it was now in danger of being turned into a vice den. Ponton thought that it already had been. The card went on to say that the SSS had been formed by a group of concerned residents in order to save the district for the nation. It concluded by

24

requesting the reader's kind support.

'Where in Soho do you live?' Ponton asked.

'Wimbledon.'

'I see.' He considered pointing out what seemed to be a slight discrepancy in this, but the lady's demeanour did not encourage it.

'Do you visit Soho often?' she asked.

'No, no,' Ponton said, feeling the need to defend himself against any suggestion that he might be partly to blame for the decline of Soho. 'I am in London for a while and ...'

'Disgraceful, isn't it?'

'Absolutely.'

'What is your profession, may I ask?'

'I am a university teacher.'

'Really,' the lady said, eyeing Ponton with rather less hostility than before. 'Did you know Keats lived here?'

'Yes,' Ponton said. 'And Blake.'

'Keats the poet.'

'Yes, I know.'

'Now it's all foreigners. Greeks and Chinese. Disgraceful.'

Ponton had gained the impression from the card that the presence of foreigners was part of the unique flavour of Soho which the lady was committed to defend, but he did not point this out. He found the lady rather intimidating, and the memory of his recent whereabouts did nothing to add to his self-confidence.

'Would you care to sign a petition?' the lady asked.

'I would love to.'

While Ponton signed the petition, the lady told him about the society. She seemed to have decided that he might be a useful ally after all, and was becoming rather more affable.

'My name is Mrs Maitland ... Yes, quite, how do you do, Mr Ponton ... I am honorary secretary of the Save Soho Society and my dear husband, Donald, is the chairman. You and Donald would have a great deal in common. He is a man of academic interests himself. You must meet him. We have taken charge of the society on behalf of the decent residents of this district who are terribly concerned at what is happening here but, how shall I put it, are not terribly good at organizing themselves. It takes a special ability, you know, which Donald and I are fortunate to have. We hold regular meetings and lobby the council who seem to be quite indifferent to the plight of these poor people. Perhaps you would

25

care to attend one of our meetings as you are in London for a while?'

'Certainly.'

'Excellent. I shan't detain you any longer, then. Good afternoon to you.'

Ponton scuttled off round the corner into the safety of Oxford Street, leaving Mrs Maitland in search of her next victim. When he looked back, he saw her handing her card to a young woman with two large shopping bags and a pram. Ponton was not a man given to scuttling, but he did so on this occasion. He had a nasty feeling, however, that he was going to see Mrs Maitland again.

Four

Ponton met Sylvia for lunch, as they had arranged, at the pub where they had met the day before. He was eating something which described itself as a ploughman's lunch. It consisted of two pieces of bread the size and approximately the thickness of a pair of drumsticks, mainly crust, a small pat of butter which refused to adhere to the bread in any way whatsoever, a rectangle of cheese deemed by the manufacturers to be Cheddar, and a mound of gelatinous pickle which was by far the largest item on the plate. Sylvia was hacking her way through a steak and chips like primitive man devouring a kill. This did not appear on the menu, but had been placed in front of her without her saying a word.

She offered Ponton a forkful of steak, dripping blood, surmounted by three chips dripping tomato ketchup.

'Thank you, no.'

'You're not eating much.'

'I had a large breakfast.'

Sylvia was anxious to know what he had thought of the performance at Monty's. Ponton steered the conservation round to Mrs Maitland.

'Oh her,' she said. 'We all know her. Right old bag. She hangs around outside the clubs sometimes. Stops us when we come out. Gives us a long lecture. She tried it on Vicky once. Got a real mouthful. Shut her up for a while. Who did you see, then?'

'Pardon?'

'At Monty's. Who did you see?'

'Oh, I don't remember their names.'

'What did they look like?'

It was obvious that Ponton was not going to get through his lunch without giving an account of his adventures at the Snow

White. He told her about the girl with the teddy bear.

'Monica,' she said. 'I'm surprised that teddy's still in one piece, the belting she gives it. Some of the places she sticks it, you've got to be thankful it's got no feelings. The smell would kill it for a start.'

'How did you come to work in London?' Ponton said.

'Me? Oh, I started stripping back home. It's in the family. Mum stripped. It's not much good back home. All in pubs. Freezing cold and people trying to pour beer over you. Monty's is lovely compared to that.'

'I don't think I've ever been to Leicester,' Ponton said.

Sylvia looked at him in total amazement.

'Y'bugger,' she said, 'how did you know that?'

'Your accent. It's very distinctive.'

'Is it? I thought it was sort of nothing in particular.'

'Not at all. You have an almost perfect cardinal three. It's very unusual.'

'Have I?'

'Definitely. Say "lovely".'

'Lovely.'

'Perfect.'

Sylvia was amazed.

'I've no idea where you're from,' she said.

'Brighton.'

'Oh.' Sylvia sat peering into her drink for a long time. She was on lemon juice in the interests of her diet. It was not like her to be quiet for so long.

'What's the matter?' Ponton said.

'Can I ask you a question?'

'Yes.'

'What do you think of me?'

'I'm sorry. I don't understand,' Ponton said. It was a question he had begun asking himself, but he had not been prepared for Sylvia asking it. He suddenly felt guilty and embarrassed, as if he had somehow been dishonest with her. Which was ridiculous. He hated being put on the spot in this way. He decided there and then that he would not see Sylvia again.

'Do you think I'm stupid?'

'My dear,' he said, 'why on earth should I think that?'

'Everybody thinks I'm stupid. Do I strike you as stupid? I mean, sort of slow?'

This was his opportunity. It was not the moment he would have chosen, but never mind. No, he would say, I do not think you are stupid. Stupid is a relative not an absolute term. I think we are very different people. You have your interests, your way of life, and I have mine. It's been awfully nice knowing you and talking to you. And you've been very helpful. But we've really nothing in common, have we? I mean, we've just about run out of things to talk about already.

He looked at her. She was still staring into her drink, not looking at him. She would be terribly hurt.

'Not at all,' he said. 'What gives you the idea you're stupid?'

'I don't know. I don't always understand things.'

'No one does,' Ponton said. 'Besides, knowing when you don't understand is the mark of intelligence.' Had he really said that?

'Is it?'

'Of course.'

Sylvia didn't seem satisfied.

'I don't speak very well,' she said.

'That's nonsense.' He felt relieved. At least they had got off the topic of general intelligence and on to his own territory where he could expound sociolinguistic orthodoxy. 'We all have our own way of speaking. There's nothing wrong with yours. You can say everything you want to say, can't you?'

'I suppose I can. It's not always very correct.'

'You know,' Ponton said, getting his pipe going, 'what is acceptable English has changed drastically since I was a young man. Take the use of the modal verbs, for example. Well, to begin with, we used to call them anomalous finites in my day.'

'Oh yes,' Sylvia said, and then decided to be honest. 'What are they?' She felt pleased with herself. She would ask questions more often.

'Must, can, should, would. Verbs like that. Changed completely. "Would" and "should" especially. There's a rather nice little limerick that illustrates it. Would you like to hear it?'

'Yes please.'

'Are you listening?'

'Yes.'

'Very well.'

Ponton recited, at a volume which took Sylvia rather by surprise:

29

'There was a young lady called Hilda
Who once went out with a builder,
Who said that he should and he could and he would,
And he did,
And he bloody near killed her.'

Someone at the next table giggled. Sylvia was speechless.

'Now,' he said, in his best academic manner, 'the interesting thing is that when I was young it would have been the other way round. He would and he could and he should. Getting closer to the actuality, as it were. You see how things change?'

Sylvia started laughing.

'Is that what you tell your students?'

'I have used it on occasion. They seem to like it.'

'I'm sure they do.'

They sat in silence for a while and Ponton reached across the table and squeezed Sylvia's hand.

'Now,' he said, 'I don't want any more talk about being stupid.'

'All right.' She got her mirror out, checked her make-up and stuffed the mirror back in her handbag. 'I have to go,' she said. 'I've got a spot. I'll see Vicky for you tonight. I don't think she'll talk to you, mind.'

'You don't have to if you'd rather not.'

'That's all right.'

She leaned across the table, kissed Ponton on the cheek and left to do her spot. Ponton stayed in the pub for another hour and smoked two pipes.

Five

There was a bit of excitement at the Snow White that evening. The girls and the regular customers had all been on edge since Liz's death. The police had been round and had scared away a lot of the regular trade who could never be sure that the man sitting next to them was not a policeman, and the audience was composed mainly of tourists and out-of-towners who didn't know what was going on. Mr Smith, however, was installed in his usual seat in the front row, bag of sweets at the ready, when Vicky came on for her last spot of the day.

Everything went wrong that evening. The curtains opened to reveal Vicky standing in front of her hammock and looking even less enthusiastic than usual. Her music did not come on. She glowered behind the curtain. The music came on. The lights went out. Vicky launched a stream of obscenities in the direction of the back wall and the lights came on again. She began her act. It was clearly not going to be one of her better performances.

She was just climbing into her hammock when Mr Smith thrust a sweet at her. She scowled at him. He leaned forward and poked the sweet under her nose.

'Swive off,' she said. She had done Chaucer for A-level.

The sweet was pushed closer and Mr Smith gave her his most winning smile. She stepped out of her hammock and stood centre-stage, looking at him.

'Stick it,' she said, and climbed back into the hammock.

Mr Smith looked mortally offended and huddled back in his seat, fiddling with the sweets in his bag. Vicky got on with her spot.

Suddenly he was on his feet and clambering, sweet in hand, up on the stage. Vicky, who had reached a particularly tricky part of

31

her contortions, fell backwards out of the hammock, with one foot caught in the mesh, and landed on the floor.

'Christ,' she said.

Mr Smith approached remorselessly across the stage towards her, the sweet held out in front of him and a look of grim determination on his face. Vicky, almost naked and spreadeagled across the back of the stage with one leg in the air, wriggled violently to get free from the hammock and screamed the place down. Monty appeared around the side curtain and took in the situation at a glance. He grabbed Mr Smith, twisted the arm which bore the sweet, forced it behind his back, and frogmarched the old man off the stage and out of the club, warning him never to return unless he wanted the police set on him. Mr Smith disappeared into the night.

Back in the club, Vicky had been rescued from the hammock and was dressing and packing her things to go home.

'He won't come back,' Monty told her. 'I threatened to break his arm and stuff his bag of sweets up his arse.'

'He hadn't better,' she said. 'I won't go on if he's here. I may not be in tomorrow anyway. I've hurt my foot.'

'You'll be in,' Monty said.

Next morning, Vicky was not in.

'I'll kill her,' Monty said.

Sylvia tried to calm him down. She had missed the evening's proceedings as she had been on at the Reveille until midnight, but she had heard about it from Vicky whom she had visited afterwards to find out if she would see Ponton. Vicky had been horrible and the visit had not lasted long. She would not see Ponton.

'I'll bloody kill her.'

This was not the first time Vicky had missed her spot. In fact, she made a habit of it. She knew it infuriated Monty.

He tried phoning her. He listened for a few minutes and then slammed the receiver down.

'It's engaged,' he said. 'She's on the bloody phone. I'm going round and sort her out.'

'I'll come with you,' Sylvia said.

32

When they got to Vicky's flat, Monty started hammering on the door. There was no answer.

'She's in there,' he said. 'She was on the phone five minutes ago.'

He banged on the door again.

'Break it down,' Sylvia said.

'You what?'

'Remember Liz. Break it down.'

'Oh my God,' Monty said. He put one hand against the wall and one on Sylvia's shoulder and swung himself against the door, smashing his foot into the lock. The wood splintered and the door creaked open.

Vicky was lying on the floor naked. She looked asleep except for the little pool of blood beside her head. Her hammock was wrapped around her neck. Sylvia knelt down and touched her.

'She's cold,' she said. She got a blanket from the bed and covered Vicky with it.

Monty had turned a very peculiar colour and was slumped in an armchair.

'What do we do?' he said.

'Phone the police,' Sylvia said, and grabbed the phone.

When the police had been informed, Sylvia attended to Monty, who seemed to be in a state of shock.

'We have to wait here until they come,' she told him.

Monty nodded vaguely.

'I've never seen a murder,' he said.

'Right,' Sylvia said. 'Bugger fingerprints. I'm making a pot of tea.'

As she was going past Vicky's body, she spotted something on the floor and bent down to pick it up. She looked at it and put it back.

'Well, well,' she said, 'I never noticed that before.'

It had been lying a few inches away from Vicky's outstretched hand. It was a lemon sweet.

Six

On the night that Vicky died Eric was, fortunately for him, fast asleep seventy miles away. After watching her at Monty's, he had taken the afternoon train down to Southampton. He spent the night on a pile of cushions on the floor in a house belonging to a boy he had known at school. Eric had got on quite well with him at one time but now he was married and had a job and a mortgage and a baby, and Eric no longer got on with him. Still, he was always ready to provide a place on the floor when Eric needed it and he knew how to mind his own business.

Eric was not entirely sure why he had left London. The reason he gave was that he had come down to see his uncle, and he did in fact devote the next day to trying rather half-heartedly to find Ponton who was, unknown to Eric, in London making his first acquaintance with striptease and Mrs Maitland. Eric spent a second night in Southampton, the night of Vicky's death, and travelled back up London the next morning.

He had no idea what he would have said to his uncle if he had found him. He supposed he had really left London because of Vicky. He couldn't get her out of his head. He went to sleep thinking about her, woke up thinking about her, and thought about her all day. She haunted him. In the beginning she had been like a secret possession, like a secret picture that he could take out and look at whenever he wanted and then put away again. But now she had taken control. She kept coming into his head all the time whether he wanted her there or not. He thought a couple of days away might have helped. He thought he might even have gone to Ponton and told him everything – just to tell someone – but it was a stupid idea.

He arrived back at Waterloo at about ten o'clock. He had

enjoyed the train journey, having managed to ruin the day completely for the two old-age pensioners sitting opposite him by going into his mentally-retarded routine. It was one of his favourites. It consisted of suddenly leaning forward in his seat and staring straight into people's eyes for minutes on end with an expression of manic glee on his face. This was interspersed with periods of deep introspection which he spent picking his nose and examining what he found there with great concentration, occasionally holding animated conversations with himself and rolling and crossing his eyes, which he was very good at.

The beauty of this routine was that his victims were torn between disgust at his behaviour and pity for one so afflicted, and spent half the journey on the verge of calling a guard and having Eric thrown off the train and the other half feeling mortified by their own callousness. His victims were always carefully selected as prime specimens of right-thinking respectability and, if all went well, they left the train in a total confusion of fear, nausea and anguish. It never failed to buck him up when he was feeling a bit down.

He had left Southampton feeling thoroughly annoyed with himself. It was an act of weakness and desperation even to think of going to see Ponton. He had never liked his uncle, or any of his family for that matter, but he did not know who else to turn to. To be honest, he had got himself into a bit of a state. He had become convinced that something awful was going to happen. Anyway, a useless day spent wandering around looking for Ponton made him realize how stupid he was being, and he came back to London feeling quite his old self and sure that everything was going to be all right.

When he was back in his flat and unpacking his things and stuffing them in drawers, he came across the key to Vicky's flat which he had stolen from her handbag on the night of the party. He had not stolen it for any particular purpose. It just made him feel good to know that it was her key and that he had it. He decided now that he would use it. It was nearly twelve o'clock and Vicky would have left for her first spot. He knew her routine exactly. Up at half past eleven, throw her clothes on, over to one of the clubs and take them off. He put the key in his pocket and went out.

It was important that she should not be in the flat when he got there. That perhaps would come later. At the moment, all he wanted was to be in her flat, to look around, to sit on her bed and touch her things. He thought about how she would feel if she knew he had been there, if she knew that he could come and go in her flat as he pleased. He remembered the way she looked at him in the clubs. Perhaps he would leave something behind, or move something, so that she would know.

When he got to Vicky's flat and let himself in, he saw what Sylvia and Monty were to see half an hour later.

He sat down in a chair and looked at her. At first he did not believe it. He told himself that he was seeing things, that his mind had gone. He closed his eyes, squeezed them tight shut and gritted his teeth, and told himself that when he opened them what he had seen would be gone. He knew he could make it disappear by will power. His will power had always been tremendous.

He opened his eyes. She was still there. He knelt beside her and touched her. She was real. He sat down again and looked at her. He felt excited looking at her naked body, though she had never excited him physically when she was alive. She was important in a different way. He felt a kind of satisfaction, almost a feeling of relief, that she was dead. Now she could never change, could never let him down. She would always be as she was when he last saw her. She would always be what he had made of her.

Then he realized the implication of her death and his mind began working, spinning wildly. He thought of everyone he had spoken to, everyone he had seen in the two days since he had watched Vicky at the club. He had said nothing to anyone in Southampton. He had just told them that he was there to see his uncle. He had not mentioned Vicky to anyone. He thought of the journey back, the old people on the train, tried to remember the people at Waterloo station, the people on the tube, anyone who had looked at him, anyone who seemed to be watching him. It was no good.

He needed time to think. He knelt beside her again, closed her eyes, and looked at her for the last time. Then he locked the door of the flat behind him and spent the next few hours wandering around London. At first he kept to the streets of Soho, sat for a while in the park in Soho Square, walked down Frith Street, cut through the side roads into Wardour Street, crossed Coventry Street and sat in the park in Leicester Square.

Now he was frightened. Someone was playing some kind of

36

horrible game with him. First the woman on the swing. Then Vicky. Killed in the same way. Someone was watching him, and worse, someone knew what he was thinking. Someone was laughing at him and playing games with him.

He left the park and followed Coventry Street back to the corner of Shaftesbury Avenue, crossed into Regent Street, and up into Oxford Street where he wandered in and out of the shops and looked at the tourists. He was sure that someone was watching him and he tried to seem casual and unconcerned, slouching along with his hands in his pockets and stopping to look in shop windows like everyone else. But it didn't work. He was still frightened.

Eric kept walking, along Oxford Street, down Bond Street and into Piccadilly. It was late afternoon when he arrived back at his flat, and the police were waiting for him.

Seven

Sylvia phoned Ponton from Vine Street police station that evening.

'Vicky's dead,' she said. 'We found her this morning, Monty and me. We're down here making a statement. Been here for hours.'

'Oh my God.'

'They've got Eric here as well. I've seen him. He's being questioned. You'd better come down.'

'I'm on my way.'

Half an hour later Ponton arrived at a dirty and undistinguished redbrick building tucked into the corner of what appeared to be a builder's yard behind Piccadilly Circus. There was a blue light over the door. He thought those had gone out of fashion years ago, along with bobbies on bicycles. The desk sergeant told him that Sylvia and Monty were still making their statements and that Eric was helping with enquiries. There seemed to be a subtle distinction. As Ponton could not conceive of Eric being helpful to anyone, he assumed that the boy had been arrested.

After spending the best part of an hour sitting on a bench avoiding the attentions of a lady who was waiting to be charged with soliciting, he was shown into the office of an Inspector Wright, who turned out to be a large and rather intimidating person with a rasping accent which Ponton identified, tentatively, as Lincolnshire. Ponton introduced himself as Eric's uncle and sometime guardian. The inspector seemed inclined to disbelieve him, and spent some time establishing Ponton's identity to his satisfaction. Half the contents of Ponton's wallet were spread out on the desk where he had tipped them in an attempt to prove that he was indeed who he said he was – though why anyone should claim a non-existent association with Eric he could not imagine –

and the inspector studied them while Ponton lit a pipe and studied him.

Two things struck Ponton immediately: the remarkable hairiness of the man, and the heroic efforts which had obviously gone into keeping this adornment under control. He had the shortest and neatest haircut Ponton had even seen. His hair was thick, black and crinkly – any longer and it would have been curly – and parted in the middle. At the sides it arched well above his ears in a meticulous razor cut. Ponton was sure that it was never allowed to get any longer. He had very bushy eyebrows which met and descended some way down the bridge of his nose, a heavy, drooping face with a wide mouth, the corners turned very firmly downwards, and an impressive pair of blue-grey jowls. His eyes were partly hidden behind square, rimless lenses. Haircut once a week, Ponton decided, and two shaves a day. Or three?

The hair, which had been defeated in its attempts to take over his face, managed to express itself elsewhere. It curled around the edges of his shirt-cuffs and poked out at his throat. Here was a man who must spend a major part of his day trying to prevent himself from looking like a werewolf.

Finally the inspector seemed satisfied and returned Ponton's belongings.

'Right,' he said, 'Mr Ponton,' with the policeman's trick of giving one to understand that one's activities have been the object of attention for some time. It appeared that he was also a pipe smoker, though he favoured some unspeakable Dutch mixture which Ponton had once been prevailed upon to try. It was thin and sweet and thoroughly unpleasant. The inspector lit up and they both puffed away in silence for a few minutes. Ponton allowed time for both pipes to get themselves going properly and then enquired after Eric.

'Didn't keep you waiting too long out there, I hope?' the inspector asked, as if Ponton had never spoken.

'Not at all.' Ponton gave it a moment or two and enquired again.

'No, not arrested. Certainly not,' the inspector said. 'Helping with enquiries. One or two points that needed clearing up.'

'In connection with the young lady who was found this morning, I presume?'

'Miss Tate, that's right, sir. There've been two of them actually, Miss Tate and Miss Brennan. Two, uh, young ladies, shall we call them?'

'Yes,' Ponton said. He did not approve of this remark. He did not believe in denigrating people on the basis of their profession. He knew a number of people, some quite academically respectable, who took a dim view of theoretical linguists.

'Have you seen your nephew recently, sir?'

'Not for a number of months, no.' Ponton told the family story. The inspector seemed more interested in his abortive attempts to keep his pipe going. He was puffing away desperately and staring at the corner of his desk in a very odd manner. When Ponton had told his story up to the point of his arrival in London, he returned his own pipe to his mouth and puffed lightly to indicate that it was still going perfectly.

The inspector was still staring in an equally odd way at Ponton and then back at the corner of his desk. There was a wire tray on the desk with a number of files in it. When Ponton had sat down, the tray had been sticking out over the edge of the desk and the files were sitting in it higgledy-piggledy. Not any more. The sides of the tray were now perfectly aligned with the sides of the desk and the files were piled up one exactly on top of another. Unfortunately this was not all. A couple of pens, an eraser and a box of matches, which had been scattered about the desk, were now lined up in military order along the front. And the inspector was looking decidedly put out.

Ponton was aware that he did this sort of thing, though never until afterwards. No doubt there was some unspeakable Freudian explanation for his behaviour, probably associated with the anal stage of his development, which he had absolutely no desire to hear about. He gave the inspector a nice smile and put his hands in his lap.

'I see,' the inspector said, trying not to look at the improved state of his desk. 'You wouldn't be aware, then, that until this morning Mr Wells was in Southampton looking for you?'

'No, I wasn't aware of that.' Ponton smiled again. 'Was he really?' He had an uncomfortable feeling that he was giving a very good impression of a half-wit. He was thinking, trying to put times and places together. 'Would that cover the time of Miss Tate's death?'

The inspector contemplated Ponton from behind his square lenses for some time. He seemed to be trying to make up his mind about something. Ponton kept his hands firmly in his lap and smiled.

'That's right, sir. Covers it nicely. We checked up on his story. Absolutely watertight. Sleeping like a baby at the time of the murder. House full of witnesses. Lucky for him.'

'Why? Would he have been a suspect?'

The square lenses caught the light and the invisible eyes watched Ponton for a moment.

'Yes, sir, he would. He was invited to come along and have a chat with us on account of his known association with Miss Tate. Seems to have been quite a fan of hers. Several people remarked on it, including your Miss Mothersill, so we thought we'd ask him in and have a look at him. Well, we didn't get much out of him at first, then it all came out at once. He admitted to being in possession of a key to the young lady's flat. Stole it from her handbag. He was in there this morning. Straight off the train and into her flat for a poke around. He found the body, only he didn't bother telling us about it.'

'I presume he's committed an offence?'

'Several actually, sir. Theft of the key, using it to enter the flat, withholding evidence of a crime.' This catalogue was ticked off on three very hairy fingers. The inspector allowed a moment or two for the gravity of the offences to sink in. 'But I don't think we'll be taking any action. As far as the first two are concerned, the young lady is hardly in a position to complain. As for withholding evidence, well, I don't think your nephew is quite all there, do you, sir?'

'I sometimes wonder,' Ponton said. 'It's very good of you to see it that way.'

'He wasn't around when the murder was committed. That's our main concern at the moment.'

'Do you know what time she died?'

'Not exactly, sir, no. Early hours of this morning. Long before your nephew came on the scene. Your friend Miss Mothersill was the last one to see her alive. Went round to see her last night. Something to do with you, I believe. Saw a man hanging about near the doorway when she left. I'm telling you all this, sir, as you'd no doubt get it from Miss Mothersill later.' The square lenses flashed at Ponton and a hairy finger was wagged at him. 'It is confidential, you understand?'

'Of course. Could she describe him?'

'Afraid not. Never looks at men in doorways. Says it only encourages them. She's quite a character, your Miss Mothersill.'

41

'Yes,' Ponton said. He was becoming increasingly unhappy with his acquisition of Sylvia in the eyes of the police. 'Will you be holding my nephew much longer?'

'No sir. No reason to.' The inspector had abandoned his pipe. He doesn't smoke it, Ponton thought, he just plays with it. Considering the tobacco, it wasn't surprising. 'Once he's made his statement, that's it for now. He's an awkward bugger, Mr Wells is, if you'll forgive my saying so.' Ponton nodded his forgiveness. 'Unbalanced in my opinion. But I can't hold him because I don't like the look of him. He's got an alibi for Miss Tate's murder. He knew Miss Brennan, but then so did half Soho. Knew her myself. You staying long in London, sir?'

'No,' Ponton said. 'I don't think so. My term will be starting soon and I ought to be getting back. As I told you, I came up to have a word with my nephew.'

'I wouldn't bother if I were you, sir. None of my business, of course, but he doesn't strike me as the type where a word would do much good, if you know what I mean.'

'No doubt you're right,' Ponton said, 'but I'd better try.' He got up from his chair and just stopped himself in time from making a few last adjustments to the inspector's out-tray.

'Do you know what the papers are going to say in the morning?' the inspector said suddenly in a voice that made Ponton jump.

'No,' he said, and sat down again.

'I don't have to see them. I can tell you now. Striptease murderer strikes again. Maniac stalks London. Knocking off strippers. Who's next? Is any woman safe? What are the police doing about it? They'll give us hell.' The square lenses flashed. The hairy finger wagged. Ponton made disapproving noises. 'They've got a point in a way. With a case like this it always looks to outsiders as if we're running around chasing our tails. In the beginning anyway.'

'What sort of case is this?'

'Nutter,' the inspector said, jerking his pipe at Ponton for emphasis, having abandoned it for any other purpose, 'some nutter with a grudge against strippers, or women in general, or the whole bloody world in general for that matter. Anybody who's ever been to a strip show and didn't think much of it.'

'You presumably could get the membership lists, names and addresses?'

'We could sir, if we wanted to. Hundreds of them. All false.' It

42

occurred to Ponton that his was not. 'You see, basically, there are three kinds of murders. There's your domestic murder. Wife kills husband. Husband kills mistress. Very messy, if you know what I mean. Psychiatrists called in and all the rest of it. Number two, murder by an intruder. Burglar comes in, wakes somebody up, somebody gets killed. This isn't one of those. This is your third type. Nutter. No connection with the victims. Probably some party who lives in Wigan. Nips down to London for a couple of days, knocks off a stripper, quick tour of Madam Tussaud's and the Changing of the Guard, back home to the wife and kids. He could be sitting here now and I wouldn't know him from Adam. No more would you. We get them in the end, mind, but it's a long business. It's what they call a man-hunt. Knocking on doors, asking questions, everything into the computer, a lot of silly buggers confessing right left and centre, and then it's as much luck as anything else.'

'Well,' Ponton said, 'I'm sure you're right.' He stood up again. 'May I see my nephew?'

'Certainly, sir. He should be finished by now. Straight along the corridor, last room on your left.' The inspector smiled at him amiably and put his pipe in his mouth. 'Good luck, sir.'

Ponton wondered why the inspector was lying to him.

He felt he would need the luck. Eric had always given him the creeps. He could still remember him as a little boy many years ago on the occasion of his visits to his sister when she was recently widowed. Eric would sit in the corner of the room, listening to their conversation and watching Ponton like a small, malevolent animal. As the boy grew up, Ponton became aware that Eric despised him. He found this disturbing to a quite unreasonable degree. He was not a man who demanded affection. He had one or two close friends, and that sufficed. He did not approve of people who went around begging affection. However, he was aware that a number of people – women especially – thought him rather an old sweetie, and he found this very agreeable.

Eric treated him with open contempt. If the boy was amiable, as he was on rare occasions, it was tainted with condescension. More often he was downright rude. Ponton had never understood what he had done to deserve it, and had never found a way of coping with it. It upset him deeply. He was not accustomed to being despised and he simply did not know what to do about it.

When his sister died he had found himself, to his horror, nominated as Eric's legal guardian. He had carried out his duties minimally. It had been one of the most miserable periods of his life. Eric had lived with various members of the family, it being understood that Ponton, as a bachelor, was not in a position to look after him in that way. He had, however, been obliged to see the boy from time to time and generally supervise his progress. He found these interviews a torture. Usually they were mercifully brief. Eric was evasive and arrogant. He did not seem to resent Ponton's interference in his life. Rather, he seemed to enjoy the opportunity of displaying his contempt and watching Ponton's embarrassment. He enjoyed making the old fool squirm.

This was bad enough, but there were even worse times when Ponton would find the boy in a state which could only be described as manic, and he would be obliged to sit and listen to a harangue from Eric that could go on for hours. It would be impossible to convey the farrago of nonsense that would come from Eric's mouth on these occasions. It usually centred around some unfortunate person with whom Eric had a slight acquaintance. This person, who was probably barely aware of Eric's existence, might for example be madly in love with him, totally infatuated. Or then again it might be someone who hated him and was planning his downfall in some Machiavellian fashion. It was all nonsense of course. Eric had no way of telling what people were really thinking. He had no awareness of any mind but his own. It was as if his imagination were so vivid and so hyperactive that it swamped, blanked out any information from any other source. There were times when Ponton thought he was psychotic.

When he got to the room at the end of the corridor, he could see that Eric was alone inside, stuffing his belongings into a duffel bag. He looked even worse than Ponton remembered. He knew what the inspector meant about Eric being lucky to have an alibi. His nephew looked exactly the sort of person whose vocation in life might be to strangle women in the obscurer parts of London.

The Pontons were not a beautiful family. Each member carried some mark of the Lord's disfavour, with the exception of Eric who had inherited the complete set. Like all the Pontons he was a little above medium height, but seemed taller because of a raw-boned thinness which exaggerated the size of his head, hands and feet. His hair, which was sandy-coloured and stringy, was beginning to thin already though the boy couldn't be much more than twenty. He compensated for this by wearing it shoulder-length so that it hung over his ears in something resembling a pirate's ringlets. He had the family teeth – rather worse, in Ponton's opinion, than his own. He was wearing a filthy grey overcoat far too broad on the shoulders and reaching almost to his ankles, which could only belong to someone else or have been purchased by Eric out of sheer perversity. Under it were a dirty striped shirt, open at the neck and cuffs, and a pair of indescribable jeans. Ponton was not by nature a cruel man but he had often felt that his nephew should have been exposed at birth.

Eric looked up and saw him. He squinted at Ponton and bared his fangs in a way which was Eric's equivalent of a greeting.

'Hello, uncle,' he said, 'I hear you've got yourself shacked up with our Sylvia.'

This reminded Ponton of another feature of Eric's personality which he had noticed in him since childhood: the ability, with a minimum of conversation, to arouse in his interlocutor the desire to smash his face in with a blunt instrument.

'May I ask what gave you that impression?'

'I met the stripping hippo on the way in here. She says you're great friends.'

'I have a high opinion of Sylvia.'

'Don't we all?'

Eric continued packing his duffel bag. Ponton sat down. There were two chairs in the room, on either side of a plain square table. Eric was standing with his foot on one and Ponton took the other, which he presumed had been used by the policeman who had had the happy duty of taking Eric's statement. He was beginning to feel ridiculous already. He would never have let a student get the better of him the way Eric did. And why did the boy always make him feel guilty?

'I understand you found the body. It must have been terrible.'

Eric said nothing.

'You're free to go, you know. The police seem satisfied.'

'Do not leave London. Do not change your address.' Eric grinned at him. 'We've been through that already.'

'I see. I'm told you've been in Southampton looking for me.'

'I was. We all have our lapses.'

45

'I gather it wasn't important.'

'It might have been. It isn't now.'

'Because of Miss Tate?'

'Perhaps.'

Eric had finished his packing and squinted at Ponton as if to enquire whether there might be anything else on his mind.

'Do you mind if we discuss it?'

'If you like.'

'Would you mind sitting down?'

Eric turned the chair round, swung his leg over it as if he were mounting a horse and sat down, resting his chin and hands on the back. He was wearing a large ring with a purple stone and his fingernails were dirty.

'Well?' he said.

'I understand you were fond of Miss Tate.'

Eric said nothing.

'I'm very sorry. It's dreadful to lose someone you're fond of.'

No response.

'Did you know Miss Brennan?'

'Yes.'

'How did you feel about her?'

'She seemed important at the time.'

'And you were in love with Vicky?'

'That's probably what you'd call it.'

'Did she love you?'

'Don't be absurd. Have you met her?'

'No. Sylvia was going to try to arrange it.' Eric delivered himself of a kind of snort, of contempt or derision. 'I don't suppose there was time... I'm sorry. It's terrible to lose two people you know, let alone people you're fond of. It's a horrible coincidence.'

The next minute Ponton nearly jumped out of his skin. Involuntarily he raised his hands to protect his face. Eric's chair fell with a clatter under the table.

He had been perfectly calm, lounging in his chair, looking at Ponton with his usual insolence. Suddenly it was as if an electric shock had gone through him. He had jumped up and knocked his chair over. Now he was stalking around the room and glaring at Ponton.

'Are you mad? Are you?'

'I don't understand.'

46

'They both died the same way, didn't they? First her and then Vicky.'

'Yes.'

'Somebody is playing some kind of game with me. It's some kind of horrible game.' Eric walked across the room, leaned on the table, looked at Ponton and said very quietly, 'Is it you?'

It took Eric some time to regain his usual composure, if that was the word. A policeman had looked round the door twice to see what was going on, and Ponton decided they had better be on their way before someone thought of locking Eric up for the night just in case.

Ponton had tried to calm him down. He was beginning to understand Eric's state of mind. Of course he didn't believe in coincidence. He believed in conspiracies, conspiracies against him. He believed in himself at the centre of the universe and everything revolving around him. It was his mother's fault. Two women he was fond of had been murdered. Therefore they had been murdered because of him. Obviously someone was following him round and killing any woman he felt affection for. Obvious, if you were Eric.

Ponton felt that old mixture of anger and weariness coming over him which he always felt when he tried to talk to Eric. He saw the look on Eric's face. He had seen that look on other faces. People who came to his house and talked about religion, with a foot in the door. A colleague who had discovered the key to all the languages of the world hidden in the Dead Sea Scrolls. The world was full of people who had seen the truth and never needed to listen to anybody again. Unlike most of them, Eric seemed to have been born that way.

Ponton gave it one more try.

'Look,' he said, 'someone is going round London murdering striptease dancers. You happened to know the two victims. You were fond of them both. That is the full extent of your connection with the whole affair. The police are satisfied that you are in no way involved. Will you accept that?'

Eric smiled at him, that pitying smile which had always been one's reward for failing to understand Eric's peculiar logic.

'Someone is playing games, uncle.'

'Someone is committing murders. Probably some misguided

moralist who thinks he's ridding the world of sin. Eventually someone will confess to these murders, or the police will catch him, and there'll be a photograph in the newspapers of some poor mad wretch you've never even heard of. Can you believe that?'

'You don't understand. Someone...'

'All right,' Ponton said, 'I give up.' He stood up and pushed the chair under the table. 'Will you stay on in London when the police have finished with you?'

'I'll see it through.'

'You mean until he's caught? It could be a long time.'

'I'll see it through.'

'Very well.' Ponton looked at his watch. It was just after ten o'clock. 'The pubs will be open for a while,' he said. 'Would you like a drink? We can talk about something else.'

'No thanks, uncle. Why don't you see if Sylvia's still around? She might fancy a quick one.'

Ponton did not reply. He was trying very hard to feel sorry for Eric, but he couldn't. He had done his duty to the family. He had done his duty by the whole host of Pontons living and deceased. He did not care if he never saw Eric again. Frankly, he did not care if his nephew was convicted of several murders of which he was totally innocent and hanged by the neck until dead. He was sick of the whole business. He was sick of London. He would leave tomorrow and that would be the end of it.

Eight

The next morning Ponton was back at the Snow White. However, he was not there on this occasion for the purpose of watching striptease, though he had some difficulty in persuading the man at the door that this was in fact the case. He was there to see Sylvia.

He could not leave London without saying goodbye to her. He had got up early, done his packing, said goodbye to his hosts, checked the train times, and all he had to do was get in a taxi and forget about the whole wretched business. Eric would have to take care of himself. But he couldn't go without seeing Sylvia. It would have been mean and she would have been hurt. He would go in the afternoon. He phoned the Snow White and arranged to see her between spots.

It occurred to Ponton on the way to the club to ask himself what on earth he thought he was doing. He was going to say goodbye to a friend who happened to be a striptease dancer. This did not strike him as a satisfactory answer. Was he serious? He had in the past been offered, and had turned down, the attentions of women a good deal more desirable than Sylvia. This was in fact a slight exaggeration, but the argument was good in principle. In practice, women had stopped offering him anything some time ago when word had got around that he was a lost cause. He wondered if he were turning into a dirty old man. He would have to watch closely his manner of observing schoolgirls.

'When are you leaving, then?' Sylvia said.

'This afternoon. I don't think there's anything more I can do.'

'Oh. Eric all right, is he?'

'As all right as he'll ever be. The police don't seem interested in him. Neither am I, frankly.'

'Oh. That's it then.'

49

'Yes.'

They were standing in the foyer of the club, Sylvia having just finished her spot. She was wearing a robe made of towelling. It was open almost to the waist and several times too small. Her breasts were enormous. They seemed to begin just below her chin and bulged out at the sides, obliging her to stand slightly hook-armed like an amiable gorilla.

'Would you do me a favour?' she said. 'Say no if you like.'

'What is it?'

'Could you put it off till tomorrow? I need to talk to you.'

'Can't we talk now?'

Sylvia grabbed him by the shoulders and propelled them both across the foyer and into a corner.

'I want to talk to you about the case,' she said.

'What case?'

Sylvia had him pinned in the corner with his back to the door of the gents' toilet and was whispering loudly in his ear.

'The murders,' she said. 'I think we should work together. Sort of pick each other's brains.'

'Well, the police seem to think ...'

'Bugger what they think,' she said. 'They both knew him, didn't they? Liz and Vicky. They both knew him.'

'Yes,' he said, 'I think they did.'

'And the police don't think so?'

'Not according to the version I was given.'

'Well then.' This was said with such an air of stating the obvious that he didn't know how to argue. Besides, she was right. She had put her finger on something that had been bothering him since yesterday, and he did feel like talking about it.

'All right,' he said. 'When?'

'It'll have to be this evening. I can get off early.'

'This evening, then. We'll meet and discuss it. Just discuss it, all right? Then I really must get back.

'Fine. What are you doing now?'

'I don't know.'

'Why don't you have a word with Monty while you're here?'

'Why should I want to have a word with Monty?'

Poor Monty, it transpired, was deeply upset by the two murders, not to mention his lengthy interview with the police on the previous afternoon. A nice chat with a person such as Ponton would do him a world of good.

50

'He's taken it very bad,' Sylvia said. 'He's trying very hard to be cheerful.'

'I'm sure he doesn't want to see me.'

'He does.'

'How do you know?'

'Because I told him he did.'

'My dear,' Ponton said, trying to shuffle his way out of the corner, 'I'll discuss the case with you this evening, but I really don't think I want to see Monty.'

'Come in, squire,' Monty said, when Ponton's head made its appearance around his door. 'Have a pew. Cup of tea?'

Ponton noted that he was indeed trying to be cheerful.

Monty was a large, powerful man of about Ponton's age with a jovial, ugly, rather battered face and a black suit that made him look like an undertaker. Or perhaps more like a boxer who was too soft-hearted to hit anybody. Hence the face. He was sitting in a black leather armchair behind a desk covered in papers.

Ponton accepted the tea. Monty had his own gas ring and kettle in the office. It was a haven of domesticity. The foyer of the club was decorated with pictures of women in alluring poses and various states of undress, and Ponton had expected more of the same in the office. Not so. The calendar on the wall showed not women but a huntsman astride a horse, with a horn to his lips, against a background of rural English tranquillity. There was a row of trophies on a shelf. Had Ponton been right about the boxing? More likely darts, or snooker. Was Monty old enough for bowls? The armchair which Ponton sat in had an antimacassar. Plaster ducks would not have been out of place.

There was a pile of magazines on the corner of the desk. On the cover of the top one was a photograph of a girl with the largest breasts Ponton had ever seen, larger even than Sylvia's. He wondered if she was real.

'Not your taste, squire?' Monty enquired. Ponton was not sure whether he meant the girl or the tea. 'Mine neither, really. I flog this stuff on the side,' he said rather apologetically, poking one of the magazines to reveal another similar cover. Ponton averted his eyes. 'How's the tea?'

'Rather strong.' It was thick and almost black and sugared to taste, Monty's taste presumably.

'I know. I like it that way. Keeps me regular.' Monty had a good laugh about this. Ponton decided to abandon the tea and got a pipe going. 'Well squire, you were in for the show the other day. What did you think of it?'

'Very interesting.'

'It's OK,' Monty said. 'You don't have to be polite with me. Want to know what I think? Bloody awful. Lot of girls, bored out of their skulls, taking their clothes off. About as erotic as a slap in the belly with a wet fish. In my opinion.'

'So what is the attraction? It seemed very well attended.'

'Oh yes. Here every day, some of them. Two hours at a stretch. Back in the evening if they can manage it. Practically live here.'

'Well?'

'Fantasy, squire, in a word.' Monty poked the magazines again. 'I mean to say, what's actually going on up there on stage is pretty deadly, right? Nice girls, mind. I'm not saying they're not. Bored sick. Doing it twenty times a day. Six days a week. Sexually arousing as a kick in the you-know-where. Fantasy, that's what it is. Who knows what's going on in their little heads?' Monty tapped his skull. 'That's where it's all happening. They sit there looking as if they're in a bloody coma, but it's all going on up here.'

Monty tapped the side of his head again and then sat back in his chair, cradling his mug of tea. Ponton was getting sick of this. He was beginning to regret agreeing to stay on another day. The meeting with Sylvia no longer seemed such a good idea. Now that Eric was in the clear, the murders were none of his business. He certainly regretted seeing Monty. He wished he wasn't so friendly, though he suspected that the jolly humour and the bonhomie were as false as hell. Ponton wanted to dislike him. When he should have been on a train home, if he'd had any sense, here he was having a nice friendly chat with the manager of a strip club. Ponton wanted to hurt him, to see how deep the friendliness really went.

'Is that what you think the murderer is doing,' he said, 'fulfilling a fantasy?'

This was below the belt but Ponton didn't care. It had the desired effect. Monty sat forward, put his mug down, crossed his arms on the desk and rested his head on them. He was quiet for a long time. Then he looked up at Ponton.

'I wish you hadn't asked me that,' he said. 'I really do. I don't know what's going on but it frightens the life out of me. Do you know what's going on?'

52

'No.'

'I knew Liz Brennan for ten years,' Monty said, and started fiddling with his magazines.

'I'm sorry. I thought you might have some insight into all this.'

'I wish I had.' Monty was pouring himself another cup of tea. Ponton declined. 'Look, I've been in this business for years. It's harmless, right?'

'I don't know.'

'Well I think it is. I mean, if they weren't in here they'd just be out on the streets making a nuisance of themselves. Flashing their what's-its at any woman who happened to be going past. While they're in here they're not causing any trouble, are they?'

'No. Just fantasizing.'

'They'd be doing that anyway. All I do is give them something to work on. The stripping, all this,' he poked the magazines, 'it's just something for them to get their minds working on. If they couldn't get hold of this stuff, they'd find something else. Some of them could get a rise out of the phone book.'

'No doubt,' Ponton said. He was not convinced by this argument. He had heard it all his life, and it seemed to him that it could be used to justify any barbarity whatsoever.

'They rely on it, you know. If they couldn't come in here and watch the girls for a couple of hours, God knows what they'd do. Go berserk, probably.'

Someone, Ponton thought, already has gone berserk. Besides, that contradicts your previous argument.

'Look,' Monty said, 'I market a commodity, that's all. Dreams, that's what it is. Day-dreams. The girls on stage out there, the girls in here,' he fingered the magazines again, 'they're just raw material. You can make anything you like out of them. Open the pages and there they are.'

'But it's not real,' Ponton said.

'That's just it. Who wants real? Look at these.' He opened one of the magazines and flashed Ponton a picture of a naked girl sitting on a motorbike. 'These girls don't grow old. They don't argue back. They don't make demands. You open the page and there they are. When you've had enough you close it again. They're perfect. Who wants real when you can have perfect? Look, have one on the house. What do you fancy? Big tits, whips, school uniform?'

'No thank you,' Ponton said.

53

'They retail at two quid apiece, these.'

'No, really.'

'Don't kid yourself, squire.'

Monty leaned back in his chair and winked at him. That did it. Ponton got up to leave.

'I'm sorry,' he said. 'I'm not being much help. Sylvia wanted me to see you.'

Monty leaned across the desk, gripped Ponton's arm and pulled him back down into the chair.

'She's frightened.'

'Yes, I suppose she must be.'

'She's one of the best, Sylvia.'

'Yes,' Ponton said, 'I know.' Monty had not said 'your Sylvia', but that was what he meant. Ponton was reminded of Inspector Wright.

'They're all frightened. I can see it in their eyes when they come in. They're afraid to go on stage in case that bastard's out there watching them and picking the next one. They're afraid to go home in case he's round the corner. You know, when Liz died, it could have been anybody. Old boyfriend, anybody with a grudge. Nothing to do with the clubs, you see what I mean? Then, when he got Vicky as well, that was the end of that idea. No question about it. Somebody's got it in for strippers. And he's not going to stop at two, is he? Why should he? They're all bloody terrified. They still come in, though. Go up on stage, do their spot, round to the next club. They're professionals, these girls. Amazing. Me, I'd be home under the bed.'

'Yes,' Ponton said, 'so would I.'

'Why do they do it? It's not the money. They must be mad.'

There was a long silence while Monty contemplated his magazines and Ponton looked round the room at the calendar and the trophies and wondered if it was safe to attempt to rise from his chair. He was beginning to feel rather sorry for Monty, despite his determination to dislike him. Monty, after all, had not done anything to him. He seemed to be a man who would like to think he was doing an ordinary, everyday job like bricklaying or selling newspapers and suddenly he had been forced to consider the possibility that he was pandering to the fantasies of a murderer. That was the problem with the whole wretched business. He could feel sorry for Monty. He genuinely liked Sylvia. They seemed to be ordinary decent people who would be kind to animals and give up their seats to old ladies on the bus. It was the same thing that had bothered him when he saw the striptease and found it merely grotesque. There was nothing he could put his finger on and say that here, at least, was something definitely morally wrong. Or was he being naïve, was he expecting too much in asking for moral black and white? They were just a collection of averagely decent people in a rather unsavoury profession. And yet two women were dead, and if Monty was right there could be more. And surely the key to it all was here in the clubs, with the bored girls and the music and the lights and the old men with their newspapers and their heads full of dreams.

Ponton stood up.

'I'd better be going,' he said. 'Thanks for the tea.'

'Any friend of Sylvia's.'

They shook hands. Monty started going though the papers on his desk. As Ponton was going out of the door, he looked up.

'Mr Ponton.'

'Yes.'

'It's not my bloody fault, you know.'

'No,' Ponton said, 'I'm sure it's not.'

Ponton was impeded in his exit from the club by what appeared to be a picket line which had sprung up since his arrival. A row of elderly persons, including a clergyman, were blocking the doorway and eyeing Ponton viciously. One of them carried a placard which enquired whether he were not ashamed of himself. He was pondering this question when he heard a disagreeably familiar voice.

'Mr Ponton!'

Ponton looked round.

'Good afternoon, Mrs Maitland.'

'Really, Mr Ponton, I had not expected to see you here.'

'I am assisting the police,' Ponton informed her, in a flash of inspiration.

'Oh,' said Mrs Maitland, visibly taken aback. 'You've been called in?'

'You might say that.'

'Are you a criminologist?'

'Not exactly.'

Mrs Maitland barked her orders and the pickets fell back

55

reluctantly to allow Ponton through. As he looked back, he saw her smiling benignly after him.

Ponton had phoned his friends in Highgate and arranged to keep his rooms for another night, and that evening, definitely the last before his return to Southampton, he and Sylvia sat in his living room together and discussed the murders.

He had taken her to dinner at an Italian restaurant in Old Compton Street. It had been quite an enjoyable meal, although he had been annoyed by the attentions of a waiter who had clearly formed the wrong impression of his relationship with Sylvia. She had dressed for the evening with uncharacteristic decorum. She wore a long, loose dress which hinted at her ample proportions rather than forcing them on one's attention, and her make-up was restrained. She had obviously given some thought to her wardrobe, and Ponton was gratified.

She spent a lot of time talking about her boyfriends, by which he presumed she meant her lovers. There seemed to be a great number of them. Once or twice he completely lost track of which one she was talking about. Several of her relationships seemed to be in a state of minor crisis and she asked Ponton's advice, which he felt ill qualified to give. She was obviously highly promiscuous. Or rather, she was totally hedonistic about sex, regarding it as a pleasure and a nice way of getting to know people. Ponton felt a twinge of envy, and a certain amount of apprehension.

As they were leaving the restaurant, Ponton was accosted by a drunk. He had seen this person weaving his way towards them and muttering at passers-by. When he reached Ponton, the drunk stood directly in front of him, looking him up and down belligerently. Ponton stepped to one side. The drunk stepped aside and stood in front of him again.

'Lend us fifty pee, mush,' the man said.

'No,' Ponton said, 'I don't think I want to.'

He took exception to the misuse of 'lend'. He also took exception to being addressed as 'mush'.

'For a cup of coffee,' the man said.

'No.'

The man stepped forward, took hold of the end of Ponton's tie, and tugged on it.

'Y'bugger,' said a voice at Ponton's side, and the next thing he knew the drunk was sitting on the pavement with a look of utter astonishment on his face. Sylvia had pushed him, with the flat of her hand against his chest, and was now standing over him with hands on hips waiting for his next move.

The man took one look at his assailant, rolled over on to his hands and knees in something like a sprinter's starting position, pushed himself up and disappeared down the street at a speed which did him great credit considering that a few minutes earlier he had hardly been able to walk.

'Are you all right?' she said.

'Yes, of course.'

'Are you sure?' She was fiddling with his tie, trying to get it straight. 'You look a bit funny.'

'Nonsense.'

'Do you want to sit down for a bit? There's a park round the corner.'

'I assure you,' Ponton said, 'that I am perfectly all right.'

They walked on up the street to the tube station and got back to Highgate without further adventures.

They were sitting in the deep armchairs in Ponton's living room, each armed with a brandy. He had also armed himself with a large note-pad and a pencil and a copy of all the newspapers which carried an account of the latest murder. Inspector Wright had been entirely correct in his predictions concerning the newspapers.

'Right,' Sylvia said, 'where do we begin?'

'Vicky Tate. I think we could usefully pool our knowledge there.'

'OK. You start and I'll fill in the gaps.'

Ponton sniffed his brandy and took a sip. Sylvia did the same, and they began.

Nine

Vicky had finished her last spot at Monty's at about eleven o'clock in the evening. She had used the hammock. She left the club shortly after and went home, much distressed by the incident with Mr Smith. She left the hammock in the dressing room. One of the other girls had noticed it there fairly soon after Vicky left, but it had not been noticed again. Sylvia finished her last spot also at about eleven. She had not performed at Monty's since four o'clock in the afternoon. She went round to Vicky's flat, stayed briefly, and left to go home about midnight. Vicky had been unpleasant, though no more so than usual. On her way out, Sylvia had noticed a man in the doorway next to the flat. It was dark and she had not looked closely at him. It could have been anyone.

Vicky had been murdered some time between midnight and the early hours of the morning. The papers were vague about this. She was discovered shortly after noon by Sylvia and Monty, although Eric had in fact been in the flat about half an hour earlier and had chosen to say nothing about it. Her clothes had been torn off and the hammock was tied around her neck. According to the newspapers, the police had established that she died from a blow to the back of the head, as Liz Brennan had done. In Vicky's case, it seemed to have been caused by her head striking against the edge of the wash-basin in her room. There was blood on the basin. She had also received a blow, probably a punch, to the jaw. The hammock had been identified by several girls, including Sylvia, as the one which she used in her act.

The police had, as a matter of routine, searched the dressing room during the afternoon following the discovery of the body to test the theory that Vicky's hammock was still there and that a second one had been used in the murder. The hammock was not to be found, and none of the girls had seen it during the morning. Besides, as Sylvia said, there were not that many hammocks lying about. No one, however, had seen it being removed from the dressing room.

'At this point,' Ponton said, licking his pencil and turning the page of his note-pad, 'we must look rather closely at the whereabouts of the hammock. Did Vicky have another one, a spare, one she might have kept at home?'

'Not as far as I know,' Sylvia said. 'I suppose she might. It always looked like the same one, and I must have seen it dozens of times.' She was curled up in the other armchair with her shoes off, looking very much at home.

'Very well. We have two possibilities here.' Ponton was scribbling on his note-pad as he spoke. 'One. The hammock used in the murder was the same one used by Vicky that evening. In which case, it was taken from the dressing room. Two. A different hammock was used. In that case, a different problem arises. Why was Vicky's hammock removed from the club at all? And by whom? In either case, we seem to have a murderer with access to the dressing room that evening, or with an accomplice who has access.'

'Looks like it,' Sylvia said. 'Any more of this stuff?' She was waving an empty brandy glass at him. He got up and refilled their glasses.

'Well, then,' Ponton said when he had made himself comfortable again and had a sip of his brandy, 'let's assume for the moment that we are dealing with one hammock and not two. Then whoever killed her removed it from the club somewhere between eleven and the time of her death and took it with him when he went to her flat. How big is it, by the way? Rolled up.'

Sylvia indicated the size between her brandy glass and her free hand.

'A bit bulky,' she said.

'It would have to be taken out inside something. A carrier bag would do. All right, now, I'm afraid we're going to run into a problem here.'

'What's that?'

'We are going to have a number of people with access to the dressing room that evening. In other words, people with the opportunity. We are then going to have another group of people with a possible motive that we know of for murdering Vicky. And

59

unless I've overlooked something, there will only be one name which appears on both lists.'

'Who's that?'

'One thing at a time,' Ponton said. 'We haven't got that far yet.'

'Sorry.'

'Now, let's look at opportunity, that is access to the dressing room. Who do we know was definitely there?'

'The girls.'

'How many?'

'Eight. Not counting Vicky.'

'And Monty presumably?' Ponton wrote on his note-pad. Sylvia nodded. Ponton wrote again. 'Anyone else?'

'Harry.'

'Who's Harry?'

'He helps Monty with the props, Vicky's hammock and things. He's just a kid. Only been there a couple of weeks.'

'So he didn't know Liz Brennan?'

'No.'

'Anyone else?'

'Not definite, no.'

'All right.' Ponton turned over the page and made a new heading. 'Now, who else might have been there? Our amiable friend at the front desk for example.'

'He doesn't usually go backstage.'

'But he might have done?'

'Possible.'

'Anyone else? Someone must work the lights. Would he have gone backstage?'

'Possible.'

'Anyone else?'

'No.'

'Very well.' Ponton drew a line across the page. 'So we have eight women and four men with access or possible access to the dressing room. Would any of them have a motive for killing Vicky, any motive that we know about?'

'No.'

'They all got on well with her?'

'Nobody got on well with her. If she was going to get murdered every time she got up somebody's nose, she'd have been dead long before now.'

'But one name on this list does rather stand out as far as motive is concerned,' Ponton said, turning back a page. 'Monty. You heard him threaten her.'

'He threatened her all the time. Didn't do him any good. If he was going to kill her for missing her spot, he'd have done it ages ago. Besides, you didn't see the state he was in when we found her. And he was fond of Liz. Thought the world of her. We all did.'

'Somebody didn't,' Ponton said. 'But you're right. It's not very conclusive. The same can be said of all of them.' Ponton flicked his page over. 'If any of them had a motive, we don't know what it was. And we're not in a position to find out.'

'So where do we go from here?'

'We pause,' Ponton said, 'to contemplate an interesting little point. We must assume that the police are as capable of doing this sort of thing as we are.'

'I wouldn't count on it.'

'Oh, I think so. We must assume they have reached the same conclusions. Which means that our friend Inspector Wright was attempting to lead me up the garden path.'

'Jack the Ripper, you mean.'

'The nutter from Wigan, yes. I was rather surprised at the time that he should be quite so forthcoming. I can only suppose that for strategic reasons the police have some sort of official version which bears no resemblance to the facts. I don't see why he should especially want to lie to me.'

'Maybe you're a suspect,' Sylvia said cheerfully.

'Possibly.' This had occurred to Ponton and he preferred to keep it out of the discussion. He drank some of his brandy. He was beginning to find Sylvia's presence rather disturbing. Perhaps it was simply that he was not used to having someone in his rooms. He had become possessive of these rooms, as he was of his house in Southampton. He liked having his own private territory where people did not intrude. He even got upset when people came to read the meter or when postmen rang the doorbell instead of just sticking things through the letter-box. And now here was Sylvia, sitting in his armchair with her legs curled up beside her and her toes tucked down the side of the cushion and her shoes kicked halfway across the floor and a brandy in her hand, for all the world as if she were some kind of fixture.

'Anyway,' she said, 'never mind the police. Get on with it.' She had a sip of brandy and pushed her toes further down behind the cushion.

'All right. So far we've been looking at opportunity, access to the hammock. Let's look at it another way. Motive.' He started a new page in the note-pad. 'The outstanding candidate on this list, to my mind, is Monty. And, of course, he appears on the first list. But we've dealt with him, I suppose. So, Eric.'

'Why Eric? He wasn't even in London.'

'Because he was infatuated with Vicky, and possibly with Liz as well, and that provides us with a link between the two murders. Also, he's mentally unstable. However, as you say, he has an alibi, checked by the police.' .

'If you want a motive,' Sylvia said, 'how about Mr X? He gets my vote.'

'Mr X is a problematical figure, assuming he exists. Frankly, I don't believe a word of it. Miss Brennan's story is in itself rather difficult to swallow. Is it really credible that a man would pay fifty pounds in blackmail rather than let it be known that he had been to a striptease show? It's hardly that much of a disgrace these days. As for the idea that he would commit two brutal murders in order to protect his identity, I simply don't believe it.'

'Suppose he didn't want anybody to know he was in London that day? It wasn't being seen in Monty's that bothered him, it was being seen in London. How's that?'

'It must have bothered him a great deal to commit two murders. What was he doing that was so secret?'

'I don't know. It was just an idea. He still gets my vote.'

'Mr X is a dead end. We have no way of tracing him, and I don't see that the police have much hope either. The only two people who knew his name are dead.'

'Exactly,' Sylvia said. 'Go on, next one.'

'Mr Smith.'

'Harmless.'

'What about the sweet? She didn't take the one he offered her at the club, so where did it come from?'

'She must have taken it some time. Stuck it in her pocket. It fell out in her flat. It could have been there for weeks. She wasn't a great one for tidying up.'

'He did have a grievance.'

'He's also about a hundred years old.'

'Yes, I suppose so.'

'Is that it?'

'That's it. Apart from one rather strange incident. The telephone.'

'Yes,' Sylvia said, 'funny about that.'

'We know that when Monty tried to ring Vicky, her phone was engaged. We also know that by then she had been dead for several hours. Now, if Eric is telling the truth about times, he'd already left the flat when Monty phoned. That puts someone else in the flat between the time that Eric left and the time that you and Monty arrived. Who?'

'Don't ask me,' she said. 'You're the clever one.'

'I have no idea. I'd love to know what fingerprints the police found on that telephone, but I don't suppose they're going to tell me, so that would seem to be the end of that. Very well,' he said. He drew a thick line across the page of his note-pad, turned over and made a new heading. 'So much for the facts. Let's see if we can draw a couple of definite conclusions. We are considering two murders here. To start with, we must decide whether we regard them as related.'

'Of course they're related,' Sylvia said emphatically, as if it were a thoroughly silly thing to start with.

'I think I would agree with that. Apart from the link with Monty's, and the nature of their profession, there are too many aspects which we would otherwise have to regard as coincidence. The first one being that death was caused in both cases by a blow to the back of the head. And, conclusively I think, there is the similar use to which the swing and the hammock were put.'

'Sort of a trademark.'

'In a way, yes. It obviously has some significance in the murderer's mind. So, conclusion number one. The murders are related. I think we're safe there. Secondly, it seems highly probable to me that both Liz Brennan and Vicky knew the murderer. Both women were killed in their own flats late at night. In neither case is there any indication that the door was tampered with. Therefore, both women opened the door and let the murderer in. Is it likely that they would open the door to a stranger at night?'

'Around there? You must be joking.'

'All right. So, either the murderer identified himself to their satisfaction or he possessed a key, which would again indicate that he was known to them. Who kept spare keys?'

'I had one for Liz, I told you. I think Liz had one for Vicky.'

'Anybody else? Boyfriends?'

'Liz didn't have a boyfriend, I know that.'

'What about Vicky?'

'On and off. But you can be sure they didn't get their hands on a key.'

'All right. Conclusion number two. The murderer was known to both victims and they probably opened the door to him.'

'God,' Sylvia said, and shivered, 'it gives you the creeps. You realize I probably know him as well.'

'Yes, I realize that.' Ponton tried to pull his armchair over beside Sylvia's. It was too heavy to budge. He went over and knelt beside her chair, resting his hand on the arm. She put her hand on top of his. 'There are certain unpleasant facts,' he said, 'which we have to face.'

'I know.'

'This man, whoever he is, is a maniac. He'll probably try to kill again. We can only hope that the police are either very clever or very lucky.'

'Fat chance,' she said. 'Don't worry. He won't get me.'

'You must be very, very careful. Don't open your door to anyone at night. Not even if it's someone you know well.'

'I'm not that stupid.'

'One more thing. I'm not trying to interfere in your private life, but do be very careful who is in the flat with you at night.'

Sylvia laughed.

'You mean sort of go on the wagon for a while?' she said.

'Until it's over, yes.'

'I think I can manage that. If it's not for too long.'

Ponton stood up, with some difficulty, from his kneeling position.

'Would you like a final drink?'

'No thanks. I've still got a drop.'

'Well, I think I'll have one.'

He poured a small brandy, sat down in his armchair again and lit a pipe. He felt that he had failed. He had reached two conclusions, both of which were apparent at the outset, and perhaps cleared up a few points which had been foggy. And that was it. He hated problems he couldn't solve. Even more, he hated problems which were incapable of solution because essential information was missing. Was the hammock which ended up round Vicky Tate's neck the same one she had used at the club a few hours earlier or

64

was it not? Who exactly had been in the dressing room that evening? How long had they been there? Whose fingerprints were on the telephone? Was there any record of a telephone call from Vicky's flat? The police presumably knew the answers, or would find them out, so how on earth had he got involved in this mess in the first place? It wasn't his job.

The culprit was taking an inordinately long time getting through her last drop of brandy, and he began to wonder if she had taken up residence in his armchair. Of course, he had done it for her. He had felt a certain curiosity about the murders, incited mainly by the inspector's determination to tell him a cock and bull story about deranged persons from Wigan. And there was also the question of Eric's involvement, which seemed to have been settled. But mainly he had done it for Sylvia. What had she expected of him? Did she expect him to work it out and come up with a name? Probably. He had a long drink of his brandy. She was being totally unreasonable. Of course she was frightened, but what did she expect him to do about it? He realized he was getting bad-tempered and depressed, probably because he was tired. He wanted her to leave.

'I'm afraid we haven't got very far,' he said. 'It's no use pretending we're the police. We simply don't have enough information.'

'It doesn't matter. I just wanted to get a few things straight in my mind. See things a bit clearer. It's all right now.'

'Are you sure?'

'Yes.'

'Look, if there's anything I can do, you will get in touch with me?'

'OK. Thanks.'

He thought Sylvia might have made some sort of a move at this point. She didn't seem to be going to. She was still sitting in her armchair, nursing her glass, now empty, and looking at him. He finished his brandy in a gulp, got up, fiddled around with a few things in the room, took her glass off her, took the glasses out into the kitchen, came back. She was still sitting there.

'Well,' he said, rubbing his hands together and jigging about a bit, 'that seems to be that. How are you getting home? Shall I call you a taxi?' This sounded a bit rude, but it was getting late and he had a train to catch in the morning.

'Oh, I'll manage.'

65

'I'll walk you to the main road.'

'It's all right.'

He found her coat and held it out for her. She got up very slowly and looked around the room for her shoes while Ponton stood in the middle of the floor, holding her coat by the shoulders and dangling it in front of her as an incentive. She put her shoes on and backed into the coat, put her hands up and flicked her hair out from under the collar.

'You're sure about the taxi?'

'There'll be taxis about,' she said. Ponton's hands were still resting on her shoulders and she touched them as she added, 'Unless you want me to stay.'

'I beg your pardon?'

'You heard.'

'I can't really offer you ... I'm afraid I don't have a spare bedroom.'

Ponton let go of her shoulders and went scurrying round the room opening doors to show that there were no spare bedrooms concealed on the premises.

'Y'bugger,' she said, 'how many bedrooms do you need?'

Ponton said nothing. They stood looking at each other. Sylvia stepped forward, put her hand at the back of his neck and kissed him hard on the mouth, then stepped back. She took her coat off and hung it over the back of the chair, then reached behind her back and unzipped her dress. She leaned forward, stretched out her arms and shook herself, like a swimmer before a race. The dress slipped down her arms and hung at her waist. Her breasts were very white, with a tracery of blue veins.

He had seen her half naked before. In the club that morning she had been wearing a robe that hardly covered her, and now she was wearing a bra. It didn't make much difference, except that that was the club and this was here, now, in the middle of his living room.

'Well,' she said, 'your move.'

'Please.'

'Please what?' She was laughing at him, standing with her head cocked on one side and her hands on her hips. He was aware of her breathing, slow and regular.

'Please put your dress on.'

'What's the matter,' she said, 'too direct? You didn't seem to be going to do anything so I thought I'd better start things rolling.'

'Please put your dress on.'

'You did tell me to be careful who...'

'Put it on.'

It dawned on Sylvia, slowly.

'You're kidding,' she said. She stood there, trying to make out if he was joking, if it was all part of the game. She was totally unselfconscious. It made no difference to her whether she had clothes on or not.

'No.'

'Oh, come on.'

'No,' Ponton said. 'Absolutely no. I'm sorry.'

Sylvia thought about this for a while and then slipped her arms back into the dress.

'Well,' she said, quite chirpily, 'first time I've ever been turned down. I must be losing it. Would you mind zipping me up?'

'No, really, you mustn't blame yourself, I just ...'

'Don't worry,' she said, offering him her back to be zipped. 'I don't!'

Ten

Ponton had taken an early-morning train down from London and was back in his own house by ten o'clock. The first thing he did was to have a good look round to see what Mrs Thompson had been up to in his absence. She had been coming in twice a week for as long as he had lived in Southampton and took almost as much pride in the orderly state of the house as he did himself. She was an excellent woman but she did tend to move things occasionally, and Ponton hated having things moved. The house was impeccably clean and tidy and she had even bought some bread and butter and bacon and eggs for him. His pipe-rack had been moved. He moved it back.

His first duty, which he had been dreading from the moment he got home, was to visit his younger sister, Eric's aunt, who also lived in Southampton, and report his findings concerning the black sheep. She would then pass this information on, suitably embellished, to other outlying Pontons. He told her, as calmly and objectively as he could, that Eric now had a flat in Soho, spent all his time in strip clubs, was in love with a murdered girl, had been questioned by the police, and was to all appearances as mad as a hatter. This was received, as he expected, with hysteria. Ponton made it quite clear that he had done everything he could reasonably be expected to do, and was not prepared to do any more. Further hysteria followed.

Apart from this, it was a pleasure to be back. He quickly set about re-establishing his routine. He visited the newsagent on the corner to make sure his tobacco was in stock, had a haircut at the barber's where he always went and which still described itself as a barber's and not a hairdresser's, and started walking on the common again. Southampton common began about half a mile from where he lived and stretched as far as the university, where it formed one edge of the campus. If he wanted to, and he had time, he could walk home in the evenings following the common paths almost all the way. If he had a lot of time and he was feeling adventurous, he could wander off the paths and discover new ways through the trees in the wilder and more overgrown parts. He enjoyed this, provided he knew his way back to the nearest path.

On his first afternoon back, he took his usual route from the common gate – although there was no longer actually a gate, just a barrier to keep traffic out – through the cemetery and past the football pitch to the lake. There had been a lot of rain and it was muddy. The water from the lake had overflowed on to the path and a few ducks and a swan had followed it and were waddling awkwardly among the trees. The swan took exception to Ponton. It opened its mouth wide and gaped threateningly at him, flapped its wings and saw him off the premises. It reminded him momentarily of Mrs Maitland.

He refused to be upset by the swan. He set off along the path towards the wooded area of the common, telling himself once again that it was good to be back. Like the swan, he was a creature with a natural habitat and he was uncomfortable when he was out of it. He had never liked London and he was always glad to be home again. He felt as if he had been in contact with something sticky and unpleasant and he needed to get it off his clothes. He looked around him at the other people on the common. There was an old lady walking her dog, a young couple, a group of children pushing a model boat out on the lake. They were normal people going about their business, like Ponton himself, and he was reassured by their presence. They were people who had other things on their minds besides sex, and most important, they did not go around murdering one another. If Eric chose to go about with his nose in the gutter examining the contents, that was his business. And if modern novelists wanted to talk as if life were at its most real in the gutter, that was their business. He did not believe it and neither, he was sure, did the old lady with the dog.

There is a widespread opinion, no doubt one of the many ways in which Romanticism has poisoned the human mind, that anyone is capable of murder in the right circumstances. This idea has been reinforced by detective-story writers who, under the necessity of disguising their murderers' identities, have portrayed them as jolly fellows motivated by little more than a spirit of perversity. Ponton did not subscribe to this view. He did not regard himself as capable of murder under any circumstances and he extended this dispensation, out of charity and fairness, to the great majority of his fellow human beings. He believed that murderers were insane.

Recognizing insanity, of course, was another matter. And here again the whole Byronic nonsense had done its work. People expected their lunatics to be flamboyant. They looked for signs of the diabolic. Now the average murderer, when he is caught and exhibited in the law courts and the newspapers, has nothing diabolic about him. He looks like the common man who goes about his business and eats a good breakfast and watches the television like everyone else, except that he has half a dozen bodies buried in the back garden. He looks, in fact, just like you and me. Well, you if not me. Hence the assumption that he is just a common man. Hence the assumption that it could happen to any one of us.

The mistake lies in the nature of insanity. The type of madness associated with murder is not a broadening of the consciousness to allow in monsters and devils so that the poor unfortunate in question goes about rolling his eyes and tearing his hair out and generally making a public nuisance of himself. It is a narrowing of consciousness, like the narrowing of a beam of light. The murderer does not see more than the rest of us, he sees less. But what he does see is seen with a horrible and obsessive clarity. In a way, the detective stories are right. On the outside, murderers do look just like anyone else. On the inside they are monomaniacs.

Once the new term got under way, he managed to push the whole London business to the back of his mind. He had a particularly bright set of post-graduate students in his tutorials, and his own research was going well. He was working on a dictionary of linguistic terms. A recurrent problem in the literature was that people used the same word to refer to different things and different words to refer to the same thing. It was an absolute muddle and most annoying to the scholar. He was trying to impose some sort of order on it all. It was a time-consuming task and necessitated the reading of a great many grammar books, which he enjoyed. As the weeks went by, his life settled into a pleasing routine of teaching and research during the day, reading in the evenings, long walks on the common at weekends, and the occasional dinner with friends.

He had written to Sylvia, thanking her for her help and her friendship and wishing her well, and she had written back. They had both been rather trivial letters and neither of them had made any reference to their last evening together. They didn't know what to say to each other. They could hardly discuss their work. Besides, he discovered without any great surprise that she was virtually illiterate. He felt bad about her, and particularly about that last evening – he had practically thrown her out of the house – but there was nothing he could say in a letter, and he couldn't face seeing her again.

He received one other piece of news from London. Eric had apparently suffered a complete breakdown. He had gone to the police and confessed to murdering both Liz Brennan and Vicky Tate. They did not believe him. He knew nothing about the murders which he could not have got from the newspapers, and he was known to have been in Southampton at the time of Vicky's death. He told them that he had killed her by the power of his will. He was still living in London and was receiving psychiatric treatment. Ponton had been assured that he was making progress.

In Soho, life was also getting back to a routine of sorts. The girls were becoming a bit less nervous, though many of them now took the precaution of being escorted to and from the clubs by boyfriends, and the regulars were beginning to drift back now that there were fewer police about. Mr Smith, however, had not reappeared. The police had invited him to come forward. He had not done so. There was one incident, though, which took place at the Snow White about a week after Ponton's departure from London which might have struck him as significant in view of what was about to happen on his own doorstep.

Sylvia had come out of Monty's office, where she had been making free with the gas ring and kettle, and bumped into Carla. Carla made a great show of opening her handbag as if she had the crown jewels in it, took out an envelope and held it under Sylvia's nose. Sylvia looked inside. There were four or five ten-pound notes. Carla flicked them with her thumb.

'Fifty,' she said.

'Nice,' Sylvia said.

'Know where I got these, honey?'

71

'No.'

'Mr X.' Carla giggled and put the envelope back in her bag. 'You what?'

'Mr X. You know, where Liz and Vicky got that fifty. I know his name.'

'How?' Sylvia was deeply suspicious. Liz had never told anybody, not even her, and Vicky wouldn't have told Carla the time of day.

'Vicky. Vicky told me.'

'She never would.'

'Well, she did. She didn't want to but I got it out of her.'

'How?'

'Never you mind how, honey. I got it, that's all. And he paid up.'

'I don't believe you,' Sylvia said, and walked away.

When she happened to come back ten minutes later, Carla was still there. She had her envelope out again and was waving it about and telling her story to Monica, who was sitting in the corner pushing the stuffing back into her teddy bear. Sylvia would never have given Carla the satisfaction of admitting it, but the incident bothered her for the rest of the day. The more she thought about it the less she believed it.

In the weeks following the second murder, the Save Soho Society also experienced something of a windfall. Membership had almost doubled, a number of gratifying cheques had been received and the SSS card was being reprinted, edged in gold. Some members put it down to divine intervention. Mrs Maitland put it down to the murders.

'If it goes on like this,' Donald Maitland said to his wife one evening, 'perhaps we could manage to open a hostel.'

'A what?'

'A hostel. It's an idea I've had for some time. A sort of rehabilitation centre.'

'Rehabilitation of whom?'

'Fallen women.'

'Oh for heaven's save, Donald.'

Mrs Maitland had often found it necessary to warn her husband against the excesses of his own good nature. He was a kindly, rather innocent man. He had little idea, for example, of what they were actually campaigning against in Soho. He knew that wicked things went on, but his wife had thought it better to keep the details from him. He could be stubborn, though. She was a tolerant woman but there were times when he annoyed her.

'Mr Gladstone used to do it,' he said.

'Do what?'

'Rescue fallen women.'

Mrs Maitland gave her husband a withering glare. He looked back at her, sheepish but defiant. He was obviously going to be awkward. She wondered if she would not have done better to have explained the facts of life to him at the beginning of their marriage and have done with it.

'I am afraid,' she said, 'that nowadays they don't wish to be rescued.'

'There must be a few who wouldn't mind. Enough for a hostel.'

'And who would administer such an establishment?'

Mr Maitland thought for a moment.

'I have a bit of spare time.'

Eleven

The weather was awful. No matter. The year continued to fulfil its early promise. The world had been introduced to the Vietnamese boat people, and two Popes in quick succession. The party conferences had come and gone, though the general election had not. The daughter of the Prime Minister of Malta had been found guilty of throwing a bag of manure on to the carpet of the House of Commons and had paid one hundred and one pounds and fifty pence in compensation. And the Striptease Murders, as the newspapers now called them, had been temporarily eclipsed by events at a bus stop in Aldwych where a Bulgarian had been poked in the leg with an umbrella.

In the weeks that followed his return from London, Ponton found himself subject to an unaccountable change of mood. At first he was delighted to be back, back into his routine, back in his own house, back at the university, getting on with his research, and so on. No doubt his pleasure was noticeable. He had overheard a lady colleague describing him as 'a bit frisky' since his return and speculating on what he had been up to. The change came slowly and mysteriously. His enjoyment of life disappeared and he began to experience periods of depression. Admittedly his research had become bogged down, but there was more to it than that. The very aspects of his life which had always given him the greatest comfort, its orderliness and predictability, began to seem oppressive. Even the tidiness of his house became annoying to the extent that he actually spent one afternoon moving the furniture round. He found himself sitting alone in the evenings, unable to read, wishing that someone would drop by – a practice which he normally discouraged. He tried to shake himself out of it, to tell himself that it was the weather, or the fault of the long dark evenings, or the fact that he hadn't had a proper holiday for ages, or whatever. It was not a serious depression, nothing that a doctor would have recognized as such. It was a general feeling of dissatisfaction, a desire for something which he could not identify. He decided it was the London episode which had upset him. He was not sure whether it was Eric or Sylvia or the murders or the whole business in general, but something had happened and the pleasures of his life had been spoiled.

It was towards the middle of November when he heard on the university grapevine that Janet Redgrove had thrown her husband out of the house again. It was only then that he realized he had hardly seen David since his return from London. David was the one person that he might have confided in about his London adventures, but he had been away at a conference in Edinburgh when Ponton got back to the university and the moment had passed. In the last month he had seen him maybe twice at a distance and David had waved and disappeared down a corridor in the opposite direction. Ponton hadn't thought much about it at the time. He had been preoccupied with his own problems. When he heard about the latest upheaval in the Redgrove household, his first thought was to get hold of David and find out what had happened. He set off across the campus to the English department.

He had known David Redgrove for years. He was about ten years younger than Ponton, in his early forties now, and he had been at Cambridge as an undergraduate when Ponton had had his first teaching job there. Ponton had started his career in English literature but had become annoyed by the amount of sheer waffle that went on. He quickly moved to linguistics, where at least the problems were defined and one knew what one was supposed to be doing. David was one of the brightest, most likeable and most infuriating students he had ever known, and he had always retained a great affection for him. David had graduated and got his lectureship about the time of Ponton's move to Southampton, but they had continued to see quite a lot of each other until David's marriage. Ponton and Janet had not hit it off terribly well, but his friendship with David had been maintained at a distance via the occasional letter until David himself had moved to Southampton as senior lecturer in English.

75

He was in many ways the antithesis of Ponton. He was one of those men who would always look young, whereas Ponton had maintained a grizzled appearance from infancy. He had a fresh, boyish face and light, almost yellow hair which went grey very gently without anyone ever noticing the change. After twenty years he still had the appearance and manner of the bright young man just down from Cambridge which he had once been. Ponton envied him a little, perhaps, though not in any malicious way. He would probably be a professor in a few years. His books were known to the literate public, whereas Ponton's publications were known only to a select coterie of masochists. David was invited to give public lectures, which were things of great beauty. Ponton – who could think perfectly clearly – was incapable of saying anything in front of an audience without muttering and grunting and adjusting his dress and scratching himself in unlikely places and fiddling with his pipe and barking up every tree in sight. His students were used to it, but it was highly alarming to the general public. David impressed people, whereas Ponton merely made them feel that they really ought to take him home and tidy him up a bit and give him a hot meal. And yet, if he had really been given the chance of changing places with David, he would have refused. Ponton could not help seeing the world as a dangerous place where one did not go about tempting fate and one kept one's head down for fear of having it shot off. David simply assumed that the gods loved him. He saw the world as a safe and friendly place, designed for the happiness and improvement of mankind in general and himself in particular.

He had received his first come-uppance a year or so after his arrival at Southampton when he took it upon himself to fall in love with a girl in one of his tutorial groups. Ponton was appalled. David was radiant and supremely confident that Janet would understand the wonderful thing that had happened to him. He duly bounced into the house one day, informed his wife that he was in love with one of his students, who returned his feelings, and invited her to be happy for them. Janet had thrown the contents of the kitchen at him and then thrown him out of the house. The affair with the student had lasted about six months. David had survived on his own for a while, trying to work out what had gone wrong, and then Janet had taken him back. This had all happened more than a year ago and David had apparently been behaving himself since, though he appeared to have learnt nothing from the episode. He was possessed of a degree of optimism and self-confidence which Ponton found irresponsible and frightening. He expected to be happy, he expected to be successful, and he expected everyone to be delighted about it.

Perhaps it was the blast of fresh air, mixed with a pleasing light drizzle, that hit Ponton in the face as he set off across the campus which brought him to his senses and made him ask himself just what on earth he thought he was doing. The English department was on the opposite side of the campus, across University Road. Ponton's side of the road was the old side, a huddle of redbrick buildings that looked as if they had been thrown together in a hurry. David's was the new side, a sixties dream of plate glass and landscaping stretching away into the distance to merge with the eastern edge of the common.

By the time he had reached the arts faculty building and taken the lift up to the first floor, he was having serious second thoughts. It was really none of his business. David was his oldest friend but that did not necessarily mean that he would want Ponton's nose stuck into his domestic affairs. The business with the student, and Ponton's obvious disapproval, had led to an estrangement between them which had taken months to heal. Perhaps he would just go back to his office and give David a ring, perhaps arrange for them to have lunch together one day. They hadn't had lunch together for ages.

He was now in the English department, a long L-shaped corridor similar to the one which Ponton himself inhabited on the other side of the road, though in rather better repair, with doors on each side leading to the lecturers' offices. He looked up and down. There were a few students hanging about and reading the notice-board. David's office was at the end of the corridor. Maybe he wasn't in. But if Ponton knocked on the door and he was in, he was committing himself and he couldn't really pretend that he just happened to be passing.

At that moment David's office door opened and two men came out. They closed the door behind them and came plodding along the corridor, past Ponton and out through the door that led to the staircase. They stared straight ahead, taking no notice either of Ponton or the students. It struck him immediately that they were policemen. He poked his head through the door and watched them disappearing round the corner of the stairs. He didn't know why he was so sure about them. They weren't students, obviously, but they could have been staff from another department, or visitors, or anybody. Except that they weren't. They were policemen. Ponton was about to follow them down the stairs, out of sheer nosiness, when the office door opened again and David came out, with a very black look on his face. He spotted Ponton, his expression changed, and he came bounding towards him.

'Hello,' he said. 'What are you doing here? Looking for me?'

'No, not really.' Ponton started fumbling in his pockets for his pipe and tobacco. 'I had to see someone.' He looked up and down the corridor and out on to the staircase as if the person he had come to see might materialize behind him.

A girl had detached herself from the bunch of students who were standing at the notice-board, and she was now hovering beside David. Her face was invisible under a shock of frizzy hair and a pair of huge spectacles. She muttered something about an essay. David gave her a big smile as if she were the woman of his dreams, apologized to Ponton who was standing there clutching his pipe and tobacco in the realization that he had left his matches back in the office, and stepped to the other side of the corridor, guiding the girl gently across with his hand on her elbow. Ponton watched as David stood with his head bowed over the girl, his fingers still resting lightly on her arm. He wasn't looking quite as smart as usual. His normal elegance had undergone something of a modification, presumably as a result of his enforced bachelorhood. Ponton had heard that he was renting a room somewhere. It wasn't that he was scruffy exactly. He looked slightly rumpled, as if he'd been rinsed through and hung out to dry overnight. He still managed to look ten years younger than he was.

David finished his conversation with the girl, and she backed away down the corridor towards the rest of the group like a ballet dancer doing an exit. Ponton had noticed that she called him David. Students were not in the habit of calling Ponton anything other than Mr Ponton. He preferred it that way. David turned back to Ponton and gave him a big smile, though not quite the same as the one he had given the undergraduate.

'Well,' he said.

'Haven't seen you for ages,' Ponton said.

'Things have been a bit hectic.'

'So I heard.'

'Have you seen Jan at all?'

'No.'

'We're not together at the moment.'

'I know,' Ponton said. 'I'm afraid the story's all over the place.'

'Yes, I suppose it must be.'

They stood looking at each other, David with his hands in his pockets, Ponton still fiddling with his pipe, and wondered what to say next. Ponton dropped the pipe. It bounced and came to rest beside his foot. A little pile of ash fell out on the floor.

'How about lunch?' Ponton said, picking his pipe up and trying to scuff the ash into the lino.

'I can't today, Tony. I'm up to my ears.'

'Tomorrow?'

'Same story, I'm afraid.'

'How about Wednesday?'

'I have to go up to London.'

'Really? Anything interesting?'

'I might be collaborating on a book.' David smiled almost apologetically, as if he had admitted to something not quite respectable. 'It's just an idea.'

'Anyone I know?'

'Renwick.'

'Really?' The name rang a bell from Ponton's Eng. Lit. days. 'He's eighteenth century, isn't he?' David was late Romantic.

'It's just an idea. Probably won't come to anything.' David suddenly seemed rather uncomfortable and started shifting his weight from one foot to the other. 'Look, Tony, I'm sorry. I have to dash.'

'Yes, of course,' Ponton said. 'Well, keep in touch.'

'Yes.'

'Lunch some time.'

'Absolutely.'

David dithered for a moment and looked as if he might be going to say something. Ponton looked as if he might be going to say something. Then they both smiled and David disappeared round the bend in the corridor. Ponton went back to his office and worried for the rest of the day.

He could have kicked himself. He knew something was wrong. He should have said something. He should have asked what had gone wrong between David and Janet. He should have asked about the policemen. Of course they were policemen. They had that look about them. What else could they be? Bailiffs? Criminals? He pictured David's office, with the desk almost invisible under heaps of books and papers, cardboard boxes full of off-prints all over the floor, cartoons torn from newspapers tacked on the walls, and two policemen sitting there questioning him. About what?

The next day, at a time when he knew she would be home, Ponton went to see Janet.

Twelve

'I've thrown the bastard out,' she said when she opened her front door and found Ponton outside. 'This time it's for good, Tony. If he's sent you round to plead for him, forget it.'

'I saw him yesterday,' Ponton said. 'We had a brief conversation. We did not discuss you. Now may I come in?'

She stood looking up at him from her height of five-foot-nothing, with her arm across the doorway, giving it very serious consideration. Then she turned and walked back down the hallway. Ponton had been admitted.

'I suppose you want a cup of coffee,' she said.

'If it's no trouble.'

He had not imagined that it was going to be easy. Ponton's relations with Janet had always been rather strained. She was not the wife he would have expected David to choose. She was intelligent but nowhere near David's equal academically. Ponton did not regard himself as an intellectual snob, but he found the disparity odd in a marriage. Admittedly he had never understood marriages. He assumed that in this case the attraction was primarily physical, an assumption he tended to make about relationships which he could not explain in any other way. Janet was small and slight and what Ponton's heartier colleagues would have described as underdeveloped. In her thirties, she could still have passed for a girl just out of adolescence – very much the physical type that David had always found attractive. In Ponton's company she was at once unsure of herself and aggressive, almost as if she regarded him as a threat. When he and David spent an evening together talking about their work, she would sit in a corner doing her sewing or reading a novel, seemingly calm, but alert and suspicious as a Siamese cat. He knew that she saw him very much as David's friend and not hers. This was only partially true. He liked David while regularly disapproving of his behaviour. He approved of Janet but had never been able to get close to her.

Ponton sat down in the living room and lit a pipe while she went into the kitchen to make coffee. One thing in her favour was that she smoked like a chimney and he had never been made to feel uncomfortable about his pipe. He pulled a coffee table over beside his chair, found himself an ashtray and settled down to his tobacco. He liked this room. It was the sort of cosy, organized muddle that he could appreciate when he was in other people's houses, though he would never have tolerated it in his own. There were bookshelves up to the ceiling, pictures on every available bit of wall, and huge, bright-coloured cushions on the floor. His own taste in furnishings was spartan, though he had been meaning for years to buy a few pictures.

'While you're here,' she said, among the clattering of coffee cups in the kitchen, 'I might as well make use of you.' Ponton thought he was being told to help with the coffee, and was halfway out of his chair when she said, 'Does the name Reveille mean anything to you?'

He sat down again and took a moment to get a grip on himself.

'No, I don't think so. Why?' He suddenly felt extremely hot under the collar and he was glad she wasn't in the room because he had the distinct feeling that he was blushing. The Reveille was one of the clubs where Sylvia worked.

'Nothing at all?' She was still in the kitchen, shouting above the noise of her coffee-making.

'Wasn't there a magazine or something?' It was a coincidence. Of course it was.

'No, it can't be that. It has to be a place.'

She came back, put his coffee on the table beside him, settled herself on one of the floor cushions and lit a cigarette. It took him a while to achieve a satisfactorily symmetrical arrangement of his coffee mug, matches and tobacco tin.

'I can't think of anywhere,' he said. 'What's all this about?'

She sat on the cushion with her legs crossed and her feet tucked in, looking like a fasting Buddha, with her mug of coffee in one hand and cigarette in the other. She might have been no older than his students, except for the crinkliness of the skin around her eyes and mouth and on the backs of her hands. She flicked the hair out of her eyes with her cigarette hand, the one with David's ring on.

'You really haven't talked to him about this?' she said.

'No, really.'

'He's being blackmailed. I suppose it's some wretched girl.' This was announced in such a matter-of-fact way that it took Ponton a while to realize what she had actually said. She got up from her cushion and fetched her handbag, came back and sat down, put her cigarette in her mouth, rummaged through the bag and handed Ponton a sheet of paper. It was cheap, lined paper, the sort of thing that might have come from a school exercise book. The message was typed and unsigned.

Dear Mr R.
2nd instalment is overdue. Nothing has changed.
Don't be silly about this. Same arrangement.
Outside Reveille. 12 o'clock, Monday.

'Where did you get this?'

'It fell out of one of his books. I was just moving some of his books and it fell out. Something about Metaphysicals. He knows I don't read that sort of stuff. He was hiding it.' She had a drink of coffee and stubbed her cigarette out. 'It's a woman. He's buying her off. Or paying for an abortion. Probably buying her off. Abortion would be a lump sum. God knows who it is this time. Probably a bloody schoolgirl. If he had any sense he'd have burnt it. Can you imagine, sticking it in a book?'

'Was there an envelope with this?'

'No, I looked.'

'When did you find it?'

'Last Monday. He was up in London. Supposed to be seeing somebody about a book. Renwick, King's College. Do you know him?'

Ponton's pipe had gone out and he took a long time to get it going again.

'I've heard of him.'

'Well, Sunday night it was. He said he had to go up to London in the morning. This Renwick was supposed to have phoned him over the weekend, dead keen to see him, something about working on a book together. No, hang on, I'm getting mixed up.' She lit another cigarette and swayed backwards and forwards on her cushion, watching the smoke rise with half-closed eyes. 'OK, I've got it now. About a month ago, beginning of October. He said

83

he'd been talking to somebody about collaborating on a book. No name, just somebody from London. This guy was an expert on something and Dave was an expert on something and they were going to work together. Great, I said, we could do with the money. It was all a bit fishy at the time. He kept saying nothing might come of it. It might all fall through. I wasn't to get my hopes up, wasn't to bother if nothing came of it.'

'And this was the beginning of October?'

'Yes.'

'All right. Go on.'

'Well, he went up to London and saw this character. Or so he said. Apparently it was all a lousy idea. He wouldn't say much about it when he came back. Just that it was a lousy idea and he wasn't interested. And then he was supposed to have got this phone call. I suppose what he really got was the letter.'

'And this was when?'

'Weekend before last.'

'Beginning of November,' Ponton said, 'second instalment. Go on.'

'Suddenly it's all on again. Off he goes to London. This time he mentioned the name. Renwick, King's College. While he was gone I found the letter.'

'This was last Monday?'

'Yes.'

'What did you do?'

'I phoned King's and asked for Renwick. Said I was trying to get in touch with Dave and I thought he might be there. He said he hadn't seen him in over a year. Never heard of a book. I said I must have got my lines crossed and not to worry about it and hung up.'

'Then what?'

'The bastard came home. Monday night. He was just getting started on some long story about the book and I stuck that under his nose.' She pointed at the letter.

'What did he have to say?'

'Nothing. Absolutely nothing. I went clean mad, Tony.' Ponton could imagine. 'I let him have it. Both barrels. He wouldn't tell me a damn thing. Told me not to worry. Can you imagine? He's up in London paying off some woman and I'm supposed not to worry. I told him he could either explain exactly what was going on or pack up and get out.'

'And?'

'Nothing. He just kept saying it was all over. It wouldn't happen again and I wasn't to worry. So I threw him out. I don't know where he is and I don't care. I won't have it. He's got away with it once. I won't put up with it. What do you think?'

'I think you're entitled to an explanation,' Ponton said.

'I think I'm entitled to a decent husband.'

She got up and went upstairs. He heard a door slam. Ponton sat and waited for her to come down again, assuming she was coming down. After a few minutes he heard her moving about. A door opened and another one closed. A toilet flushed. She came back down. She looked as if she might have been crying.

'I'm sorry about that display,' she said. She lit a cigarette.

'That's all right.'

'I suppose it's the male menopause or something. I don't know what's the matter with him. He has to prove he's still attractive to women. Young ones. I try to understand. He just won't grow up. Why can't he accept what he's got?' She stubbed the cigarette out.

Ponton got up from his chair and stood in front of her and took her hands between his. He felt guilty because he had never really liked her, and because David was his friend and David was behaving abominably. He also felt guilty because he hadn't told her what David had said about going up to London and he knew he wasn't going to tell her.

'I'll find out what's going on,' he said. 'We don't know for sure that this has anything to do with another woman. It could be anything.'

'Don't just find out.'

'What do you mean?'

'You'll keep it between the two of you. Tell me.'

'I promise. I'll tell you everything I find out.'

He thought of putting his arm round her. Why? Because he'd just told her another lie? He decided she wouldn't want him to. It would be a totally false gesture and she would know it. She didn't trust him and she probably never would. She was standing awkwardly, stiffly, allowing him to keep his grip on her hands, not looking at him.

'All right, as long as you tell me. One of you.' It was as if she regarded him as some sort of accomplice of David's.

'I'd better be going,' he said. 'I'll be in touch. I'll see myself out.'

'I'm perfectly capable of seeing you out,' she said, pulling her hands away. He got the impression that she took a certain pleasure in seeing him out.

Ponton nearly phoned David twice that afternoon and then changed his mind, and it was evening before he actually made the call. He kept telling himself that he had promised Janet and so he had do something. But he knew that wasn't really the reason. It was nothing to do with Janet. If it hadn't been for the one word 'Reveille' in the note he would never have tried it. He would have let David go wherever he was going and tackled him when he got back. It was that one word that made all the difference.

Judicious questioning at the university had told him where David was staying. It was one of a row of houses in one of the older and seedier parts of Southampton belonging to a colleague, vaguely known to Ponton, who managed without any apparent strain to combine the functions of Milton specialist and slum landlord. It was normally let out to hordes of undergraduates, half a dozen to a room. He hoped none of David's students was there. He found the number in the book and rang. He had decided to do it by telephone so that if David even half agreed to the plan, he could put the phone down and pretend they'd been cut off. Judging by the noise on the other end of the line, the phone was communal. He asked for David. Someone went to look for him. Finally Ponton heard his voice.

'Hello?'

'Hello, it's Tony.'

'Yes?' He sounded rather annoyed.

'I wondered if you were still planning to go up to London tomorrow. You did say tomorrow, didn't you?'

'Yes.'

'Look, David,' Ponton was doodling madly on the pad beside his phone and trying to convince himself that he wasn't doing something he would regret, 'I've got an idea. I've been meaning to go up to London and see some people at University College. The phonetics people. Tomorrow's as good a day as any. I don't have any classes. I thought perhaps we could go up together. Have a chat on the train. What do you think?'

'To be quite honest, I don't feel much like chatting at the moment.'

'I'd appreciate it, David.'

He took a long time to answer.

'If you like.'

'What train are you catching?'

'Ten past ten.'

'Fine. I'll meet you at the station at ten. Is that all right?'

'I suppose so.' There was a long pause and Ponton began to wonder if he was still there. 'Tony?'

'Yes?'

'You haven't seen Jan, have you?'

'No. Why?'

'It doesn't matter.'

'Tomorrow, then. Ten o'clock.'

Ponton rang off before David had a chance to change his mind, then poured himself a brandy and sat smoking his pipe and wondering what on earth he was getting himself into.

Thirteen

The next morning Ponton was up early. He had his breakfast, which consisted of tea, toast and marmalade, a soft-boiled egg (place in cold water, bring to boil, leave precisely two and a half minutes after water starts to bubble) and a pipe. He checked that all the doors and windows were locked and the heating switched off, checked it all again, left a note for Mrs Thompson, and was down at the station before ten o'clock. He bought a day return to Waterloo, had an altercation with the ticket inspector, who was one of those persons who seem to regard passengers as a kind of parasite on the healthy body of the railway service, and went through on to platform one to wait for David. It was still only five to ten.

Southampton is one of those unpleasant stations where a red and yellow plastic façade has been stuck on to the old skeleton of blackened stone and brick. Ponton wandered up and down the platform and watched the Portsmouth train come and go. David had not appeared. It was a dismal morning, cold and grey and threatening rain. He went into the buffet and bought a cup of coffee. He wondered whether he shouldn't buy himself a sausage roll to go with it and poison himself and have done with the whole affair. He was not happy about the day's adventure.

His plan was that on the journey up he would make discreet enquiries about David's marital situation, from the point of view of a concerned friend, ask a few questions about the proposed book, twitter on generally, and try to extract a confession of what was going on. Failing this – and he expected it to fail – when they got to London he would pretend to go his own way while in fact he would head for the Reveille club and wait for David's arrival. He had no doubt that that was where David was going. Here the first problem arose. Ponton was not sure where the club was. He had the impression, from his memory of his conversations with Sylvia, that it was in Frith Street, but this would have to be checked. And there wouldn't be much time to check it. He didn't know why he was so sure about where David was going. He had no reason to be sure, but he had known from the moment Janet had shown him the note which way things were leading. He had the feeling that events were accumulating around him, that he was somehow part of it, and David was part of it, and they were both being swept along towards some awful conclusion.

The London train arrived among a great deal of clattering and banging and people rushing about. Ponton came out of the buffet and David came running on to the platform, his face bright and his hair brushed, with a smile of greeting and apologies for being late. In that moment Ponton realized something that he had known for twenty years but never admitted until now. He remembered David as an undergraduate, arriving for tutorials, usually late, with the same apologies, and he remembered the excitement he always felt and the anxiety that for some reason David might not come. He had been in love with David all those years ago. Janet had known it straight away and that was why she had never trusted him. He felt an enormous relief that he had finally admitted it to himself, and he hoped it gave him a justification for what he was going to do.

They found a second-class smoking compartment with four empty seats in a corner. David put his briefcase on a rack and they settled themselves in. David didn't smoke but there was no question of Ponton getting through the journey without several pipes. He noticed that the briefcase was bulging, no doubt filled with all the necessaries for a day of academic discussion at King's. Of course Ponton should have brought one himself. It was bound to look suspicious.

The train was somewhere between Eastleigh and Winchester when Ponton, who had been gazing out of the window for several minutes, turned and looked at David.

'Bonkers,' he said.

'Cuckoo,' David said.

'Crackers.'

David had started it. They had said everything possible there was to say about the weather – it was now raining in a steady drizzle – and Ponton had made a few hesitant attempts to direct the conversation towards something more significant, all of which had proved abortive, when David settled himself back comfortably in his corner with a wicked grin on his face, slanted his legs across the gap and put his feet up on the far end of Ponton's seat.

'I was thinking the other day,' he said. 'This may interest you as a linguist. Have you ever remarked what a wonderful collection of words there are in English to describe insanity? And the interesting thing is that they're not really derogatory terms. They're gentle, affectionate, almost terms of endearment. You know, potty, dotty, loony, loopy, that sort of thing. The English love lunatics.'

'The English love eccentrics,' Ponton said. He knew exactly what David was up to. 'Besides, are there really all that many?'

'A couple of dozen. I made a list once, in the interests of science. And mad and eccentric are the same thing. It's a question of degree, of attitude.'

'Nuts,' Ponton said.

'Nutty as a fruit cake. Batty. Bats in the belfry.'

Then they stopped and thought about it for a while and Ponton had said bonkers and David had said cuckoo and Ponton had said crackers and then they both stared out of the window and thought about it a bit more.

This was not, of course, the conversation they were supposed to be having. It was rather clever of David. He knew that if there was one way to get Ponton off an undesirable subject it was to give him the opportunity to go ferreting about in the recesses of the English language.

'I was sorry to hear about you and Janet.' Ponton gave it another try. 'I thought things were going so well. Scatty, by the way.'

'They were,' David said. 'Screwy. Dippy, dotty. Have we had dotty?'

'I think so.'

'Are you keeping count?'

'No. Look, David, you can tell me it's none of my business but ...'

'Don't you think it says something about the English perception of reality? It is a bit Whorfian, isn't it? Is that the right word?'

'Not really. Whorfian has to do with structures, not vocabulary. Look, I don't want to interfere ...'

'I mean to say, round the bend, up the pole, round the twist,

90

other languages don't have anything like so many. What do you make of it?'

'I don't know.'

'Would you agree that English gives formal recognition to the fact that we're all mad, more or less?'

This was too much. He was perfectly aware what David was up to, and no doubt it was all deliberate provocation, but that didn't mean he was going to let him get away with any nonsense he liked.

'No, I would not. I'm not mad. You're not mad, though you may be pretending to be. That poor wretch who's killing girls in London is mad.'

David took this without batting an eye. Ponton was watching.

'You are a bit eccentric, Tony.'

'I am an elderly don,' Ponton said. 'I'm supposed to be eccentric. It's expected. Anyway, eccentric is one thing and raving mad is another.'

'You've got a screw loose. Other people are off their rockers.'

'Exactly. The language makes a distinction. What you're suggesting is that there's no qualitative difference between a homicidal maniac and a man who makes models of the Houses of Parliament out of the cardboard bits inside toilet rolls.'

'I'm saying it's a continuum.'

'Rubbish.'

The matter was not discussed any further, and neither were David's domestic arrangements, except somewhere around Clapham Junction when Ponton took his pipe out of his mouth, said 'cracked', and put it back again.

'Cranky,' David said. 'Gaga.'

At Waterloo they walked to the underground together and took a northern line train. David chatted happily about this and that. Ponton had given up all hope of extracting information. Plan B was in operation. They travelled together as far as Charing Cross where they said goodbye, wished each other a fruitful day, and David got off.

His intention, he said, was to walk along the Strand to King's. Ponton supposedly intended to stay on the train as far as Goodge Street and then walk to University College. Neither was going to do any such thing. Ponton's plan was to get off at Tottenham Court Road, walk into Soho, locate the Reveille and find somewhere which allowed him to watch whatever goings-on there might be without being seen. David would probably do one of two things. The most likely was that he would simply stay on the platform and catch the next train. In this case, Ponton would only be a couple of minutes ahead of him and would have to move fast. The other possibility was that David would walk from Charing Cross to Soho, which would give Ponton plenty of time to establish himself in hiding somewhere. He had to work on the first assumption, that David was just behind him.

When Ponton came out of the underground at St Giles Circus it was raining quite heavily. It would be. He disliked Oxford Street at the best of times. He disliked it because he didn't understand what it was for. There wasn't a single shop in the whole of its length where a normal person could buy anything that a normal person might conceivably want to buy. For example, a tin of decent tobacco. It was typical of London, that vast apparatus which exists for some purpose which has nothing to do with ordinary life. It was obvious that nobody lived here. In places where people live there are shops where you can buy shoe-laces and dog collars and sacks of potatoes and hot pies to take away and tins of decent tobacco. And you cannot buy tea-towels with the Union Jack on or giant beefburgers or postcards of the Queen Mother, for the excellent reason that no sane person would wish to possess them. Ponton looked around him like a stranded missionary in pith helmet and knee socks and sensible shorts, surveying the antics of the natives on some South Sea island where the word of God had never penetrated.

Such thoughts, however, did nothing to further the business of the moment, which was to discover whether the Reveille was in fact in Frith Street or somewhere else where it had no business being. He put his umbrella up, tucked his head into his collar and made his way through the crowds. He turned left into Soho Street, crossed Soho Square, struggling to keep his umbrella up against the rain which drove at him horizontally across the open space of the park, and went down Frith Street. The Reveille, thank God, was where he had thought it was. It was on the left near the corner with Old Compton Street.

He had a look inside. There didn't seem to be anyone about. A notice outside said that the club opened at twelve, continuous performances from twelve thirty, all lovely young girls etc etc. He looked at his watch. It was now ten to. He realized that he was standing in the middle of the pavement, gawping about, obstructing passers-by with his umbrella and generally making a bit of a spectacle of himself, with David perhaps only a few minutes behind him. One man on his way down the street gave him a conspiratorial look, obviously assuming that Ponton was hovering about anxiously awaiting opening time. The sooner he got out of sight the better. He looked around for somewhere suitable. There didn't seem to be anything. Ideally he wanted to be on the opposite side of the road, well hidden, with a clear view of the entrance to the club. Unfortunately this meant that anybody standing in the doorway of the club also had an excellent view of him. He was obviously going to have to look further afield, and time was getting short. He crossed Old Compton Street, went along in the direction of Wardour Street and darted inside the best cover he could find, which was a pornographic bookshop. It said 'welcome' outside in half a dozen languages. Two of them were wrong.

His vantage point in the shop doorway, with his head poking out through a curtain made of strips of coloured cloth, was not a very good one. He could just see the end of Frith Street. If David was walking from Charing Cross, he might come through Trafalgar Square and Piccadilly and straight past Ponton's hiding place. If he had caught another tube and got off at Leicester Square, or if he was walking up Charing Cross Road, he would probably come into Old Compton Street at the other end and Ponton might see him as he turned into Frith Street and then again he might not. If he had followed the same route as Ponton, he would come from the Soho Square end and Ponton wouldn't see him at all. He might in fact come from any direction whatsoever. Ponton decided he had better change his hiding place. Besides, he was obstructing legitimate traffic in and out of the bookshop and attracting the attention of the proprietor.

It was now over ten minutes since he had left the tube station. He walked quickly to the next corner, nearer the Reveille, after having a good look up and down the street, and stationed himself in the doorway of a tobacconist's specializing, appropriately enough, in the sale of pipes and cigars. He was now much better placed. He was opposite the corner of Frith Street and he could see the door of the club and a little of the street beyond. He was beginning to wonder whether he hadn't misunderstood the whole thing, whether the Reveille of the note wasn't some other place entirely, when David walked right past him, almost close enough to touch. It gave him a terrible shock. He stood for a moment unable to move, hoping that David would turn and see him and the whole business would be over. He didn't. He stood on the corner with his back to Ponton, waiting to cross the street. Ponton edged through the door and into the shop and bought a tin of tobacco, keeping an eye on David through the window.

When he came out of the tobacconist's, David had crossed the road and was on his way into the Reveille. Ponton huddled in his doorway and watched. David was out of sight for about a minute, then he came back out again and stood on the pavement looking up and down. Ponton waited. There were crowds of people about, most with umbrellas up, and cars parked on both sides of the road. David would need very sharp eyes to spot him, tucked into the shelter of his doorway.

The person David had presumably asked for came out of the club a few minutes later. She was a tall coloured girl whom Ponton thought he might have seen somewhere before. She was wearing a light summer dress, which revealed long expanses of milk-chocolate arms and legs, and the garish make-up which Ponton recognized as the badge of the striptease profession. She threw out her arms in exaggerated mock delight at seeing David, dipped under his umbrella and kissed him on the cheek. In high-heeled shoes, she was a little taller than him and he had to raise his umbrella to cover her. They stood for a while, talking, and Ponton edged forward out of his doorway for a better view. He couldn't see them very clearly now because a group of men had gathered outside the club, reading the notice and peering inside. The girl seemed to be doing most of the talking, though, squirming under David's umbrella and waving her arms about.

The men moved on up the street and the girl was gone, back into the club. David was still standing on the pavement outside. She was back out in a couple of minutes, with a fluffy red coat over her shoulders and a red umbrella. She put her umbrella up, slipped her arm through David's, and they set off up Frith Street towards Soho Square. Ponton came out of his hiding place, crossed the street and followed, keeping well behind them on the other side of the road. He couldn't see them clearly because of the parked cars on their side, but he followed the umbrellas, one black and one red, bobbing along above the car rooftops. At the end of Frith Street they crossed into the park. Ponton crossed the road, ducking down

94

behind a couple of parked cars, slunk along beside the railings of the hospital, and sheltered in the entrance of a bank which faced directly on to the park.

In the middle of Soho Square there is a black and white building of disagreeable appearance and mysterious purpose which Ponton had stopped under briefly on his way across the park half an hour earlier. It reminded him of something from his childhood. One of his aunts had had a bird-bath in her garden with a similar structure, though in miniature, perched on the edge of it. She used to put scraps of bread inside. Ponton thought of Eric and wondered whether insanity ran in the family. David and the coloured girl were sheltering under the eaves of the bird-house. The park was deserted except for a few people hurrying across. Ponton remembered it as a rather pleasant place – he had sat there one afternoon in September, before he had ever heard of the striptease murders – with people sunning themselves on the benches and pigeons strutting about waiting to be fed. Now it looked like some abandoned back-yard with the trees black and almost bare against the muddy sky.

David and the girl were arguing. At least, the girl was. Ponton could see that she was shouting, with her face a few inches away from David's, though he couldn't hear anything. He stood and watched them through the mist of rain and shivered and lit a pipe. David seemed to be staring straight ahead and occasionally saying a word or two, which made the girl even angrier. Suddenly she opened her umbrella and set off across the park towards the mouth of Frith Street. David waited a moment and then followed her a few steps behind. He caught up with her at the corner, there was another argument, and they disappeared round the wall of the hospital. Ponton gave them a few seconds to get well ahead – he knew where they were going – and then followed them back down Frith Street, at a safe distance on the other side. They stopped at the door of the Reveille. The girl seemed to have calmed down and they were talking quietly with their heads close together. There was nowhere to hide here, so Ponton slanted his umbrella towards their side of the road, hiding his face, hurried past, crossed Old Compton Street, and took up his position again in the doorway of the tobacconist's. The conversation seemed to be over. David was walking slowly back up Frith Street in the direction they had come, and the girl was on her way back into the club.

Oh God, no she wasn't. She had turned round, looked straight at Ponton, and was now heading across the road towards the tobacconist's. Ponton stood stock still with his back to the road and his head enveloped in a cloud of tobacco smoke, taking a passionate interest in the contents of the shop window, and waited for her to go past. He had no idea where she was. He told himself it was sheer accident. She had no reason to suspect that he'd been following her. She just happened to have crossed the road. It was ridiculous to panic. He had just decided that she must be well past by now and was thinking of turning round to have a look when the girl's reflection appeared beside his in the window. She was standing about a foot behind him in the entrance of the doorway and admiring herself in the shop window. She had a long, horsy face, rather ugly, and short tightly-curled hair that looked as if it might have been a wig. She stood for a while looking at herself in the glass.

She was a highly disturbing presence, and it wasn't just because he'd been spying on her for the last fifteen minutes. She would have been disturbing anyway. He didn't know whether it was her blackness, or the mask-like face in the window, or the faint smell of her perfume like the musky smell of an animal. He suddenly realized where he'd seen her before. She had performed at Monty's that day months ago, the day after he had first met Sylvia. She hadn't been nearly so disturbing then. She had stood on the stage completely naked in front of him and she had not been a threat. The girls on the stage had existed in some sort of dream. They were safe. Now she was standing behind him in the street with her clothes on and her physical, sexual presence was almost overpowering. He would have been afraid to turn and look at her.

She was still admiring herself. Then she put the umbrella down in the corner of the doorway, teased out her hair with her fingers, pouted at her image, wiggled inside her dress and smoothed it down over her hips, pressing it close to her flesh. She looked directly at Ponton's reflection, which was staring at hers in the window with a goggle-eyed look on its face. Their eyes met. Ponton attempted a smile. The girl looked at him, formed her mouth slowly into a kiss, smacked her lips noisily with a shake of her head, laughed, picked up the red umbrella and set off down the road towards Wardour Street.

Ponton watched her for a little way to see if she looked back, then shot across the road and off in pursuit of David. He thought he'd lost him for a moment, until he saw the umbrella bobbing along ahead of him.

Ponton turned the corner of Bloomsbury Square into Southampton Row. It was now seven or eight minutes since they had left
Frith Street and he was feeling abominably cold and wet and
thoroughly fed up. They had passed a number of pubs and his
glimpses of the fuggy warmth inside had done nothing to improve
his mood. David was ahead of him on the other side, walking
quickly in the direction of Russell Square. The rain was lighter
now but there was more of a wind so that whichever way he turned
his umbrella the rain managed to blow in underneath. His trousers
were soaked. His only consolation was that David was presumably
in the same condition. And where the devil was he going? Ponton
had followed him from Frith Street into Oxford Street and across
into New Oxford Street. He wondered if they were both to be
treated to a stroll around the British Museum. They were not.
David had headed briskly into Bloomsbury. He seemed to know
where he was going. Presumably it wasn't far or he would have
taken a tube.

They were in an area of small shops, hotels and restaurants. It
still didn't look much like the real world, still peculiarly London,
but it was better than the West End. One or two of the shops did
seem to sell some sensible things. The crowds were thinner here
and he was able to keep David in view from a safe distance. He
nevertheless managed to be looking the wrong way, and struggling
with his umbrella which was in danger of blowing inside out, at the
moment when David vanished.

Ponton knew to within two or three doorways where he must
have gone. He put his umbrella down – the thing was more trouble
than it was worth – crossed the road, and walked slowly towards
the point where he had last seen David, checking each place as he
passed. The first possibility was a restaurant. The tables were set
for lunch but there didn't seem to be anyone inside. He looked at
his watch. It was nearly a quarter to one and he realized how
hungry he was. He hadn't had a bite since breakfast. He peered
into a couple of shops. Next was a hotel. He couldn't see anything
from the street so he pushed the glass doors open and poked his
head round. He still couldn't see anything except a staircase and a
lift. He edged a little way inside until he saw David standing at the
reception desk, and then backed out again into the rain.

He stood under the awning of an Indian delicatessen and
considered his options. One, forget the whole thing and go home.
That seemed rather feeble after he'd come this far, though it was

not without its attractions. Two, very clever this, book into the hotel himself, which had the virtue of getting him out of the rain, think things out and see David some time later in the afternoon. No, that was just delaying the evil hour. Three, take the bull by the horns and do something positive instead of just standing there with rain dripping down the back of his neck.

He put his umbrella up again and crossed the road to the post office, looked up the hotel number and rang. Yes, Mr Redgrove had just checked in. They put him through to the room. David took a long time to answer. Probably having a hot bath. It should have given Ponton a chance to work out what he was going to say, but he just stood listening to the ringing at the other end of the line and hoping he wouldn't answer at all. David answered. Ponton muttered something into the phone.

'Hello, Tony,' said a cheerful voice, 'I thought it might be you. I hope you didn't get too wet.'

'No, I ... well, yes.'

'Where are you?'

'In the post office.'

'Over the road?'

'Yes.'

'Well done. Look, there's a little restaurant just opposite you. Can you see it? Why don't you settle yourself in there and I'll be along in ten minutes. We can have some lunch. All right?'

Ponton was still trying to think of something to say when the line went dead.

Fourteen

'When did you suspect?' Ponton said, buttering his bread roll. It was one of those swollen round ones with a thick crust that shatters into crumbs, and cotton wool inside. The waiter had lifted the rolls carefully from a basket with a pair of tongs. Ponton wondered what he'd used to put them in.

The restaurant was empty except for one other couple in the far corner. At least it wasn't one of those elbow-to-elbow arrangements. It was a long narrow room like a railway carriage with seating down both sides – tables for four and high-backed seats which gave a good deal of privacy. David had come bouncing in, after nearer twenty minutes than ten, and obtained the immediate attention of the waiter, who had been ignoring Ponton with a surly expression on his face. Ponton had that effect on waiters.

'Last night,' David said, 'when you phoned.' He was studying the wine list. 'It all sounded a bit thin. Bit of a coincidence. I guessed you were up to something. You were rather good, I must say. I only spotted you twice. What do you fancy? Something white?'

Ponton agreed to something white. He didn't usually drink at lunch-time but he felt he deserved it. David ordered the wine and the waiter disappeared. They were having soup of the day, followed by lamb chops for David and fish for Ponton. David looked cheerful, perfectly at his ease, and above all dry. Ponton was very conscious of his trousers clinging soggily to his legs and dripping water on the floor.

'You saw Jan, I suppose?' David said.

'Yes.'

'And the note?'

'Yes.'

'There's one thing that bothers me, Tony. How on earth did you get ahead of me? One minute you were on a tube and the next you were hiding in a doorway in Soho. That was the trickiest bit, by the way. I nearly looked straight at you. You can't have followed me from Charing Cross?'

'I knew where you were going.'

'How?'

The waiter arrived with the wine and went through the whole rigmarole of displaying the label, opening the wretched thing, sniffing the cork, having it tasted and declared fit for human consumption, taking great pains not to disturb the non-existent sediment and so on and so forth, all very characteristic of a country where you're expected to play with the stuff rather than drink it. They sat back and let him get on with it.

'It was the note,' Ponton said when the ritual had been completed.

'That wouldn't have told you anything. Unless you have an encyclopaedic knowledge of the sleazier establishments of London.'

'It doesn't really matter how I knew, does it? Just accept that I'm not quite such an old fool as I look.' It was the first point Ponton had managed to score and he relished it. The wine and the warmth of the room were making him feel a bit better. And his trousers were beginning to dry out.

'I accept that graciously,' David said, and raised his glass in a salute. Ponton did the same. 'Very clever of you, anyway.'

'Who was she?' Ponton said.

'Who?'

'The coloured girl.'

'Carla Drummond. Mean anything to you?'

'No.'

'Wonderful. I've found something you don't know.'

'You're under no obligation to tell me anything,' Ponton said. 'You know that.'

'I rather feel I am, after you've followed me halfway round London in the pouring rain.' The soup arrived. It was packet mushroom. They drank the first few mouthfuls in silence. 'You remember a couple of years ago I had a relationship?'

'I remember you abandoned your wife and seduced a student.'

'Stated with your usual precision. Did I ever tell you about her?'

'Not really.' They had hardly seen each other while David

was living with the girl.

'She had this amazing face, Tony. She used to sit in my lectures in the front row. I could hardly think for looking at her. She was very young. First year. Just out of school. And this amazing face.'

The soup bowls were removed and the main course arrived. Ponton's fish was unrecognizable under a nasty-looking white sauce. David's lamb looked much better. Ponton tasted his fish. It lived up to its appearance. He refilled the wine glasses and ate some roll and butter. David was busy separating a piece of lamb from the bone.

'You were talking about the face,' Ponton said.

'Right. Pure seventeenth century. Incredibly white skin. Innocence and sensuality. Have you ever seen a face like that?'

'No.'

'Take my word for it. Very young, very pure. But there was something about the face. I don't know. A sort of heaviness around the eyes and mouth that said she'd done everything. Or wanted to do everything. Innocence and absolute sensuality. That was Victoria. It was an illusion, partly. She was a virgin.' David carefully separated meat from bone, put a piece of lamb in his mouth, chewed and swallowed. For some reason it struck Ponton as obscene.

'What happened?'

'It ran its course, I suppose.' And what on earth, Ponton thought, does that mean? 'I was infatuated, obsessed.' David had another piece of lamb. 'I wasn't entirely wrong about the face.'

Ponton was about to ask just what the point of this conversation might be when it began to dawn on him. David was tucking into his chops with his head bent over the plate. Ponton put his knife and fork down and had a long gulp of wine. He was afraid to ask.

'We're not talking about Vicky Tate, are we?'

'I always called her Victoria.'

'I don't give a damn what you called her.' He must have shouted because at the other end of the room the waiter turned round and gave him a filthy look. Ponton lowered his voice. 'Are we talking about Vicky Tate, the girl who was murdered?'

David looked up and grinned.

'That's right.'

'My God.'

Ponton had been a complete idiot. He'd been so disgusted with David at the time that he hadn't even remembered the girl's name, if he'd ever known it. He'd never asked what happened to her. He'd always assumed she was still at the university. The whole episode had been so unworthy of David, he'd just wanted to pretend it never happened. He wanted to pretend the girl had never existed.

The food was taken away, Ponton's almost untouched. David was studying the menu again, looking at desserts. The couple from the corner had left and they had the place to themselves. Ponton lit a pipe and settled himself more comfortably with his back to the wall and his legs stretched out along the seat. Desserts were a serious matter with David. He had always had a passion for them. He was finicky about food and wine, and fairly abstemious, but he always insisted that every meal should be topped off with a large helping of the most unspeakable goo on offer. He never put on weight.

The perusal of the menu went on. It gave Ponton time to recover from his shock. In the last two days he had racked his brain for every possible explanation for what was happening, for the police, the blackmail. It had never occurred to him.

David opted for the banana split.

'Are you sure you won't have anything, Tony?'

'I'll wait for coffee.'

'Look, Tony, I want to get one thing absolutely straight. I don't mind you following me. I was rather glad you were there, actually. It was rather comforting to have you plodding round behind me, darting in and out of doorways.' Ponton said nothing. 'But it's all over. The whole business is settled. Finished. That's what this morning was about. It's like a great weight off my shoulders. I feel wonderful. Don't spoil it. Don't moralize at me, Tony. I couldn't stand it.'

The banana split arrived. Two halves of banana were perched on the sides of a large oval dish with thee scoopfuls of ice-cream in the middle, all covered in cream and a thick chocolate sauce with nuts in.

'You're not seriously proposing to eat that?' Ponton said.

'Absolutely.'

Ponton gave him a moment to savour the first mouthful of banana split.

'Tell me about Vicky.'

'Victoria. What about her?'

102

'How did it end?'

'It was just over. One of those things. She agreed. I mean it wasn't just me. She absolutely agreed it was over. I tried to persuade her to stay on. She left just before the first-year exams. I knew she was in London. I never knew what she was doing. I wanted to keep in touch, find out how she was getting on, but there was Jan. She wouldn't have it. She said it had to be a complete break. I didn't have any choice.' He looked at Ponton and waited, for support, sympathy, encouragement. Ponton sucked on his pipe and appeared to be studying a poster of the French countryside on the opposite wall. 'Are you listening to me, Tony?'

'Go on,' Ponton said. 'I can't bear to watch.'

David had another mouthful of ice-cream. He was a quarter of the way through it already.

'The police came. At the university. No uniforms. Very discreet. Nobody knew. When she died they'd started checking up on her and they got to me.'

'Yes,' Ponton said, 'I think I saw them.'

'When? The other day? That was the second visit. They were on to me long before that.'

'So what did you tell them?'

'The truth. More or less. I told them it was over. We'd had an affair and it was over. She'd left the university. I hadn't seen her for ages. I didn't know where she was. They obviously thought I was a complete bastard but they believed me. I managed to keep them away from Jan. I'd been at the conference, you see. In Edinburgh. Last week of September, the week she died. Four hundred miles away. I could prove it. It frightened the life out of me, Tony, I can tell you. I was damn lucky. If I hadn't been able to prove where I was, it doesn't bear thinking about.'

'No,' Ponton said, 'you were lucky.'

'I knew she was dead. I'd read about it in the papers. It was dreadful. She meant a lot to me, Tony. I was having kittens about Jan. It was in all the papers. On the television. She never made the connection. Student called Victoria, stripper called Vicky. I don't think she ever knew her surname. It wouldn't have mattered really, I suppose, but we'd have had to talk about it. It would have raked it all up again just when it was over and done with. Look, Tony, if you don't stop making me talk for a minute, I'm never going to finish this thing.'

Ponton sat and smoked his pipe until the banana split was finished. David leaned back in his seat and gazed up at the ceiling.

'That,' he said, 'was sensational.'

'Next question,' Ponton said.

'Coffee?'

'Yes please.'

David's plate was removed – it looked as if it had been licked clean by a cat – and the coffee was served.

'Next question,' Ponton said. 'What didn't you tell the police? You are being blackmailed, aren't you?'

They both drank their coffee slowly, and Ponton continued his study of the French countryside. David was sitting hunched over the table, turning his coffee cup round and round in the saucer. Ponton could see him out of the corner of his eye.

'When I was on my way to Edinburgh, I spent a few hours in London on the way up. Just to break the journey. It was pure accident, Tony, I swear. I was walking along the street and there she was. Victoria. I literally bumped into her. We had a coffee somewhere, that's all. We just went somewhere and had a coffee. I asked her how she was. She said fine. She had a job. I didn't ask her what she was doing. I thought she looked a bit slutty. We talked for half an hour. I couldn't tell the police, could I?'

'Why not?'

'Because it would have made the whole thing so bloody complicated. I'd told them I hadn't seen her. I'd given them an alibi. I'd persuaded them there was no need to talk to Jan. If I'd said I'd seen her a week before she died, they'd have wanted to know why. They'd never have believed it was an accident. The whole thing would have got completely out of hand. I just couldn't stand all the bother, Tony. It was so much easier just not to say anything. It didn't make any difference. I couldn't have told them anything.'

'And this girl, Miss Drummond?'

'Carla. She saw us together. Do you want some more of this?'

The waiter, who had come leaping across at David's signal with the bill in his hand, was persuaded of the need for more coffee.

'Carla,' Ponton said.

'I wish you'd stop prompting me, Tony. It's getting on my nerves.'

'Sorry.'

'She was in there having coffee. She came over to the table and said something to Victoria. Had a good look at me. I'd never seen her before. God knows how she found out who I was. Maybe it was the book.'

'What book?'

'One of mine. I had it with me. I gave it to Victoria. I just felt like giving her something. I wrote some silly message in it. Anyway, Carla phoned me at the university, a few days after Victoria died. I'd just read about it in the papers. I'd just got back actually. It was the first week of term. I was feeling pretty low, Tony. I mean, one minute I was sitting there talking to her and the next ... I was fond of her, Tony. I know you don't believe that.' The fresh coffee arrived. The waiter slipped the bill under Ponton's saucer and made his escape. 'I didn't know who she was at first. It was all very crude. I suppose she was trying to be subtle or sinister or something. It just came out as crude and vulgar. She said she'd talked to the police but she hadn't said anything about seeing us together because of course I would have told them that. I had told them, hadn't I?' He mimicked Carla's voice, deep and throaty. 'She wanted fifty pounds to forget she'd seen us. I was supposed to meet her in London with the money. We went to a pub. She was incredible, Tony. She sat there and held my hand and said how upsetting it must be for my wife. She knew I had nothing to do with the murder and she wanted to spare me. She held my hand, Tony. She was very calm. Very friendly. Very chatty. Incredible.'

'But for heaven's sake,' Ponton said, 'you had nothing to fear. You had an alibi.'

'It seemed the easiest way out. It wasn't much money. It was all getting so bloody complicated. I just wanted it over and done with. I didn't want any more questions. I didn't want Jan dragged into it.'

'So you paid her?'

'Yes.'

'You didn't imagine that was the end of it?'

'I did actually.' David looked across the table at him and smiled. It was a smile that Ponton knew only too well, the one that said yes, I know I've been silly, I know I've behaved like an idiot, but that's the way I am. That smile had been getting David out of trouble for as long as Ponton had known him. 'When the letter arrived I couldn't believe it. Second instalment. There was no mention of instalments. It was fifty pounds. One payment.

105

Finished. I came up and saw her again. She didn't bother pretending. It was regular blackmail. Fifty a month for ever or she'd start writing anonymous letters. The police, Jan, everybody. I didn't know what to do.'

'If you'd told the truth in the first place,' Ponton said.

'I know, Tony. If I'd told the truth in the first place it probably wouldn't have mattered. But I hadn't. I'd lied to the police. I was getting in deeper and deeper and I didn't know how to get out. So I paid. I didn't know what else to do.'

It was this sort of helplessness, Ponton remembered, that he'd once found so attractive. The little boy lost. Ponton as the wise old tutor and David as the young student with brilliant ideas who could never quite get to tutorials on time. It had never occurred to Ponton until this minute that it was somewhat less attractive in a man of forty.

'So why did you change your mind?' he said.

'Did I?' David looked inside his coffee cup and put it down.

'I got the impression today's meeting was unscheduled.'

'Jan found the note. That was the first thing. There was a blazing row and she threw me out. Then the police came again. They asked me the same questions. I told the same story. I knew I couldn't go on. For one thing I couldn't afford it. That's when I decided to come up again and finish it.'

'And is it finished?'

'Yes. I told her she could go to hell and write to anybody she liked. She won't, or I don't think she will. She doesn't want a lot of trouble. She just wants money. She said she wasn't in it alone. She had to talk to somebody. A boyfriend. She wanted twenty-four hours. I told her to go to hell. I said I never wanted to see her again and I never wanted to hear from her again. I don't care what she does. It's all over now and I feel wonderful. It's been like a nightmare. I feel in control again.'

'Why the hotel?'

'I couldn't face going back just yet, back to that bloody awful house. I thought I'd stay up here for a night, have a look at the bookshops, see a show. I've stayed there before. I'll go back tomorrow.' David leaned back in his seat and patted his stomach. 'Tony, do you think we could get out of here? I rather feel the need to walk this lot off.'

Fifteen

David sat on his bed in the hotel room. It was the only comfortable
thing to sit on. There was one chair in the room, a low padded
thing with no arms, but the back was broken. He had thrown his
jacket over it when he came in and the back had wobbled a bit and
looked as if it might fall off. He fetched a pillow out from under
the bed cover, propped it up against the headboard and lay back
with his hands behind his head. They had switched on the neon
sign on the wall of the hotel opposite and the greenish light
flickered across the ceiling.

After leaving the restaurant, he had walked Ponton round
Bloomsbury Square a couple of times and then returned to the
hotel. They had intended to sit in the gardens for half an hour and
finish their conversation but it was too wet, even though the rain
had stopped. The benches were soaking and all the trees and
bushes were still dripping rainwater. The whole place looked
thoroughly depressing, so he had taken Ponton on a brisk trot
round the gardens and then they had separated, Ponton returning
to Waterloo and David to the hotel.

He felt guilty about Ponton, but only a little. Admittedly it had
been rather cruel to drag him around London in the rain, but the
sleuthing had been Ponton's idea. Nobody had invited him. Once
David had realized what he was up to, he couldn't resist it. The
opportunity of leading Ponton through Soho and in and out of
strip clubs was too delicious to pass up. He probably didn't know
what a strip club was. Ponton was one of those people who think
that anyone with an IQ over a hundred and ten couldn't possibly
be interested in sex. The confession in the restaurant had been
unpleasant – his confessions to Ponton always were – but he felt
he had an obligation. He seemed to have spent half his life

confessing various bits of misconduct to Ponton. He felt like the henpecked husband in picture postcards, creeping back home from the pub. The image of Ponton in curlers and armed with a rolling-pin popped into his head and wouldn't go away.

He still hadn't managed to work out how Ponton had got ahead of him. When David had got off the tube at Charing Cross and Ponton had stayed on it and disappeared into the tunnel, he had begun to wonder whether he hadn't done Ponton a serious injustice and the expedition to London was entirely innocent after all. The next thing he knew, Ponton was standing with his head stuck out of a doorway in Old Compton Street. Another mystery, now that he came to think of it, was that Ponton should have made the connection between Victoria and Vicky Tate quite as fast as he did. The murder had been in all the papers, admittedly, but he didn't think Ponton read that sort of thing.

He made himself more comfortable on the pillow and pushed Ponton out of his mind. The principal thing he felt now was relief that it was all over. From the moment he first saw Victoria he had been under a kind of spell, and now it was broken. He was still a little apprehensive about Carla but he didn't think there was any real danger there. It was all a bluff and he should have called it sooner. As he had told Ponton, he was beginning to feel in control again. He had finally managed to get the idea of Victoria out of his head. It had taken a long time and it hadn't been easy.

He still remembered the first time he saw her, sitting in the front row at one of his lectures, turning the pages of her notes with long, thin fingers. Her wrists and hands were tiny, small-boned like a bird, and the fingers were incredibly long. He couldn't take his eyes off her. Then she looked up and he saw her face. He had pictured that face in his mind a hundred times since then – the black hair, longer than when he had last seen her in London, very white skin, large eyes, small nose, a wide mouth with thin lips – and tried to explain to himself why he found it so exciting. He never entirely succeeded. She was very young, of course, and very aware of how attractive she was, but it was more than that. It was a face that combined purity and sensuality in the most startling way. It was the face of a flagellant nun.

He proceeded slowly with his seduction of her, making a fuss of her in tutorials, taking longer to go through her essays, and eventually inviting her out to dinner. She received these attentions with a kind of passive resignation which gave him no indication of how much progress he was making. He began visiting her room. She had an attic in a big house overlooking the common. It was here that he discovered something which was to excite and infuriate him in the weeks that followed. She would not allow him to kiss her. She sat on the edge of the bed and turned her head away, offering her cheek or her neck but never her mouth. If he tried to force her, she fought and bit him. He was getting thoroughly fed up with this performance when he discovered that her reservations did not extend to being taken to bed. They began sleeping together regularly, whenever they both had a free afternoon.

The taboo on kissing remained. It drove him wild. It was frustrating physically, but above all he was enthralled by the idea of it – the idea of a girl who would go to bed with him and make love with him and not allow him to kiss her on the mouth. At first he thought it was just a kind of peculiar physical squeamishness, or perhaps a way of keeping him interested. If it was that, it certainly worked. If she had refused to go to bed with him, he supposed he would have lost interest eventually, despite the face. If she had given in to him completely, she could never have achieved the power over him that she gained by withholding this one silly, trivial thing, a kiss on the mouth. But it was more than that. It was neither a whim nor a piece of adolescent cleverness. It was a way of giving herself and not giving herself. It was a sign almost of contempt.

She wouldn't talk about it. She wouldn't give him any explanation. Her attitude was that he had the rest of her body and so there was nothing for him to complain about. He began to worry away at the problem as if it were a literary puzzle or a difficult piece of research. Victoria became his consuming interest. He watched her and listened to everything she said, trying to put clues together.

The explanation, when he finally managed to make sense of her conduct, was perfectly simple if rather bizarre. She had decided that it was time she was seduced and that he would do as well as anyone. She had reached the age when a seduction was appropriate. It was a necessary experience. David had been selected because he had a certain status, or because she just fancied someone older, or for whatever reason happened to be in her head at the time. The kiss was another matter. That was being held in reserve. Without the kiss, their love-making was meaningless. It was an experiment, a stage in her development. She was giving him nothing that mattered. The kiss was the real emblem of her virginity. He didn't know where she'd got the idea from. She'd probably read it in a book.

The first time she kissed him, they were out for a walk on the common. They were standing arm in arm by the lake and she turned towards him quite suddenly and kissed him on the mouth. It was that afternoon that he told Janet he was in love with Victoria and she was in love with him, and Janet threw him out of the house.

They lived together for a term and the following vacation. It was not an altogether happy time. The virginal sensuality which had so attracted him was not the only expression her face was capable of. It was replaced more and more often by sullen petulance or a stubborn, smouldering resentment when she failed to get her own way. She was still capable of behaving like a child and he always forgot that she was little more than a schoolgirl. Absurd practical jokes like hiding his trousers in the fridge sent her wild with delight, and she would jump up and down and cry and bang her fists against the wall with excitement if he found them and tried to put them on. At other times she was morose and would hardly speak to him. She had a ferocious temper which could flare up at any moment with no warning and no apparent reason, and disappear just as quickly. She was quite simply impossible.

The process by which he fell out of love with her was a gradual one and he was only vaguely aware of it happening. The image of Victoria which he had created for himself in their first few weeks together was impossible to sustain in the face of the particular human being – lovable, inconsistent, infuriating – whom he was living with. He tried to remember how she had looked to him the first time he saw her, but the image would no longer fit. Victoria had become simply Victoria. It was as if he had gone to sleep and dreamt of a timeless love goddess and then woken up to find himself living with a bad-tempered and demanding adolescent. He began to compare their tawdry attic room with the house he had left, the house with his books and pictures in it, the house which was now Janet's. He had stopped being invited to dinner parties. Some of his colleagues were hardly speaking to him at all. He had given up a great deal for Victoria, and there was very little recognition of it on her side.

Their parting had been mercifully civilized. There had been a

110

great deal less emotion than he had expected. She had taken it very well. Perhaps she was even tired of the affair herself. He had offered her money, which she had refused. She still attended his lectures for a while, in the back row, and then one day she was gone. He had wanted to find out where she was, but Janet had delivered her ultimatum and that had seemed to be the end of it.

It had been a terrible shock to see her again in London after all that time. He had been walking along the street, thinking about the paper he was going to deliver in Edinburgh, and there she was standing in front of him. She had seen him first and was watching him, suspicious, hostile, frozen like a startled animal. He had taken her somewhere and bought her a cup of coffee and they had talked for half an hour and he had nearly fallen in love with her again. She looked awful, with a lot of cheap jewellery hanging off her and far too much make-up, but her face was the face he had seen the first time she ever looked at him. The spell was beginning to work again.

A week later she was dead. The first thing that occurred to him was that this was a signal, a message to him that he had been released, that the spell was broken for ever. It was as if she had died in order to set him free. It was an insane idea but it took quite a hold on him for a time. Then everything had started to go wrong. The police had come and he had panicked and told them just enough to get rid of them and keep them away from Jan. And then there was Carla, Carla who had involved his wife, Carla who had sat and talked to him and held his hand, calm and friendly and evil, Carla the last persistent link with that whole episode of his life.

He reached out and turned on the bedside light. It had grown dark while he was lying there. He got up from the bed and stood looking out of the window, watching the passers-by on the street opposite. The pavements were sleek and shiny but there were no umbrellas about now. The people looked cold, huddled in their overcoats, but dry. He put his jacket and coat on and went out.

Ponton had had a rotten journey back to Southampton. He had caught the stopping train, which took an hour and a half, and the only available seat was a non-smoker. He arrived in a state of serious tobacco withdrawal and treated himself to a taxi home. He settled himself back in the seat and put a pipe in his mouth, whereupon the driver had cordially thanked him for not smoking.

He put the pipe away.

The sight of his own living room, exactly as he had left it, revived him. He had a pipe, put the fire on, made himself a plate of bacon and eggs and a pot of coffee and had another pipe. He put his pyjamas and dressing gown and slippers on. He had been sitting around in wet clothes all day. He was probably going to catch pneumonia. He could feel it coming on already. And all for what? For the pleasure of discovering that his closest friend, a man he had admired for twenty years, had the moral sense of an alley cat.

It wasn't really a new discovery. If he was honest, it was partly the alley cat in David that he'd always liked and admired, and envied perhaps. There had been moments during the morning's pursuit through the streets of Soho which had been quite exhilarating, a kind of vicarious participation in whatever David was up to. Ponton sometimes wished he had been born an alley cat, but he hadn't and that was that. He was more of a squirrel, fussing about up and down his tree, whiskers a-twitch against the scent of intruders, and worrying himself silly over whether the nuts would see him through the winter. He consoled himself with the thought that there was a need for squirrels. A world full of alley cats would be unbearable, though there was no doubt they had a better time of it.

David, for example, had seemed thoroughly pleased with himself that morning, scoffing ice-cream like a schoolboy. He was being blackmailed, his wife had thrown him out, he'd lied to the police about a murder, and he seemed to be revelling in it. He was getting things under control and he knew it would all come out right in the end. Alley cats always know they'll survive with the loss of a tuft or two of fur at the very worst. Ponton, on the other had, who had no real involvement in the business at all, was worried sick and expecting to be arrested at any minute.

He couldn't escape from the idea that the whole wretched affair was creeping closer and closer. It had started with a silly conversation in a pub, and then there had been the second murder and Eric's involvement and the dreadful evening with Sylvia. These things had happened at a distance but the distance was ever decreasing. It was becoming more and more difficult to remain an observer. The last time he had just about managed to come home and get back to work and re-establish his routine and put it all behind him. This time it was going to be impossible. From the

112

moment he saw David standing on a street corner in Soho talking to that woman, something had changed. The murders had really touched him for the first time and his immunity was gone.

He got up and washed his plate and pottered round a bit and decided to give himself an early night. He checked that the windows were shut and the doors bolted, mucked his pipe out and left a pipe-cleaner in it to keep it dry overnight, and went to bed. He was sure he wouldn't be able to sleep. He was wrong. He was fast asleep in ten minutes.

He might not have slept so soundly if he had known what was about to happen in Soho – something which would seem significant later, though no one except Carla took it very seriously at the time.

Sixteen

Carla had come home from her last spot of the day and found Thomas already in the flat. This was unusual as it was still half an hour until the pubs shut. He grunted and then ignored her. He was being difficult. He'd been in a filthy mood since the afternoon. After her conversation with Redgrove, Carla had done her first spot at the Reveille and then found Thomas, dragged him out of the pub and told him what had happened. He took it badly. He looked as if he might be going to hit her, but there were people about so he went into a sulk instead. He was still in it.

'I'm going out,' he said, when she'd been back about five minutes. She knew what that meant.

'Bring it back and drink it here,' she said. 'I don't like being left on my own.'

She had kicked her shoes off and was sitting watching him, hunched up in the chair with her arms folded round her legs and her chin resting on her knees. Thomas snorted and put his coat on. It was the short black leather one she'd bought him for his last birthday. He had looked wonderful in it then, and he knew it. He'd strutted round in it for days, even in the hot weather. It didn't look quite as good on him now. It was tight when he belted it round the waist because he was getting a pot belly from too much beer. She had not pointed this fact out to him. He was vain about his looks.

'I'll be fifteen minutes, then,' he said.

'Sorry, honey. I just don't like being here on my own.'

The door slammed.

She sat staring at the door and listening to his footsteps down the corridor. She heard the street door bang. A few minutes later it banged again. He must have forgotten something. She listened

114

for his footsteps. There was nothing. It must have been the people upstairs. She didn't know why he was making such a fuss. They'd never really expected it to work, or at least she hadn't. It had been a game, like Liz and Vicky and Mr X.

She'd been suspicious as soon as she'd seen Vicky having coffee with Redgrove that day. She'd never seen him before and he didn't look like anybody connected with the clubs. He looked as if he had money, but not in the way that Carla sometimes had money. If she had it, or Thomas had it, it burnt their fingers and they went out on a binge and blew the lot. He looked as if he just drew it out of the bank every week and never gave it a second thought. Carla watched as he wrote something in a book and pushed it across the table. Vicky took it and put it in her bag, without looking at it. She was doing her virgin schoolgirl act. It got under Carla's skin. Vicky got under her skin most of the time.

In the evening she found an excuse for dropping by Vicky's flat and she had a good look round while Vicky was in the loo. The book was lying on the floor. Carla had her hands on it straight away. She flicked through the pages. 'To Victoria', it said, 'with all my love, David'. She turned it over. There was a photo of him on the back cover, the author, Redgrove, and some stuff that told her who he was and where to find him, if she ever needed to. Carla stored the information away. By the time Vicky came back from the loo, she was curled up in an armchair looking all innocence and the book was back on the floor.

When Vicky was killed, Carla had told Thomas about Redgrove and they decided there might be something in it. Besides, Vicky had been a cow while she was alive. She might as well do somebody some good when she was dead. Carla had phoned him at the university and suggested that he might want to keep his meeting with Vicky secret, for a price. She was astonished when he agreed to pay up, and even more astonished when it worked the second time. It was amazing how much people had to hide if you just started digging a little. She seriously thought about picking people at random out of the phone book and ringing them up and asking for fifty quid to keep quiet about what she knew, without being too specific. But it was too good to last. She wasn't at all surprised when Redgrove had turned up at the club that morning and said it was over. She'd screamed at him and threatened him, but that was for show. There wasn't much else she could do. If Thomas had imagined it was going to last for ever, he was more of a fool than she thought.

He was back in a lot less than fifteen minutes. There was a furious kicking on the door. It took her by surprise because she hadn't heard him come along the corridor. But she was used to the kicking. He came back with a crate of beer in his arms and couldn't be bothered to put it down to get his key out. This time she didn't feel like getting out of her chair to let him in. She shouted at the door.

'Open it yourself.'

The kicking continued. She shouted at him again, louder. More kicking. Lazy pig, she thought, and got up slowly from her chair.

She opened the door. He wasn't there. She looked outside but she couldn't see anything because the light had gone in the corridor. It had been going for days. It was one of those strip lights that flicker on and off and make a sort of buzzing noise before they pop. She'd told the landlord about it ages ago. The only light she had on in the flat was a little lamp in the far corner and it wasn't strong enough to make any difference to the gloom in the corridor. She stepped a little further out and looked towards the staircase. She didn't go far from the doorway because she didn't have any shoes on.

It was a first-floor corridor with two flats. Carla's door was about halfway along, on the left as she stood facing the stairs. The other door, behind her on the right, led to an empty flat. The corridor ended just beside it in a blank wall. The stairs at the far end led down to the street door on the right and up to the next floor on the left. The corridor ahead of her was pitch dark, but she could just make out the gap in the wall where the stairs were. She moved forward a little and shouted.

'Honey? Is that you?'

There was no answer. She opened her mouth to shout again when it dawned on her what was happening. Suddenly she felt cold. She was aware of the thinness of her dress and her bare arms and the rough, gritty feel of the floor against the soles of her feet. Thomas wasn't there. She was standing in the middle of a pitch black corridor and somebody had been banging on the door and that somebody wasn't Thomas. Whoever it was, he was still there, somewhere in the darkness around her. She knew she had to get

116

back inside the flat and shut the door but she was afraid to move.

She began to shuffle backwards and sideways towards the door, sliding her feet across the floor. He was there somewhere, watching her. She thought that as long as she moved slowly, stealthily, he would not touch her. He was waiting for the sudden move, like an animal watching for the sign of fear. She reached out behind her and found the edge of the door with her fingers, and in that moment she knew where he was. The door was wide open. He had slipped into the flat behind her. He was in there waiting for her.

Her only chance was the street door. She looked at the gap in the wall at the end of the corridor and tried to think of the distance to the top of the stairs, to remember how long it took her to get there from her door. Five seconds? Ten seconds? He was in the flat waiting for her. If she started to run, by the time he heard her she would be at the top of the stairs. Turn right, down the stairs, through the door into the street. If the door was open there would be enough light from the street to see the stairs. She remembered she'd heard it bang shut. They would be dark. She knew she had to run but she couldn't move. Her legs wouldn't work. She willed herself to run, pictured herself running. Then she heard the noise behind her and felt the cold touch of his fingers on her neck. Somewhere she heard the noise of beer bottles clanking. She screamed.

Thomas was halfway up the stairs when he heard the racket. He started to run, two steps at a time, with the beer crate held out in front of him. He wasn't sure what happened next but somebody or something came round the corner at the top of the stairs and straight into him. He dropped the crate and went sprawling on his face on the stairs. The street door banged behind him. He struggled to his feet. There were broken bottles all around him and he cut his hand. The stairs were slippery with beer. Somewhere up above him he could hear Carla still screaming.

117

Seventeen

Ten days after his trip to London, Ponton opened his Sunday newspaper and read of a cyclone which had killed fifteen hundred people in Sri Lanka, an increase in the television licence fee, a military coup in Bolivia, and the appearance of the former leader of the Liberal Party at Minehead magistrates' court. There was also an article on the Striptease Murders. That was all he needed.

He had got up late, cooked himself a large breakfast, eaten it, tidied up a bit and settled down to read the papers. He hadn't even bothered to get dressed yet. He was having a lazy day. He was determined not to think about London, or the murders, or David, or his work – certainly not his work.

The dictionary of linguistic terms was not going well. He was having an inordinate amount of trouble with the word 'morphophoneme'. He'd been stuck on it for days. This was absurd. It was not as if he were in any doubt as to what the wretched thing was. He had been on terms of the greatest intimacy with a wide variety of morphophonemes for more than twenty years. He knew one when he saw one. If there was any man qualified to distinguish a morph from a phone from a morpheme from a phoneme from a morphophoneme, then Ponton was that man. The precise and accurate use of terminology, even to the point of obsession, was his trademark. If there had been any improvement in recent years in the writing of linguistic papers – and there had been – it was in large measure because his colleagues were no longer able to formulate their ideas in a sloppy fashion without being aware of Ponton's beady eye peering over their shoulders.

Now he couldn't even think straight. His work was getting into the most awful muddle and he had neither the will nor the ability to sort it out. He was suffering from the same sense of depression

118

which had afflicted him after his previous visit to London. Only now it was worse because David had joined Eric and Sylvia among the ghosts who haunted him and sabotaged his concentration. He had not spoken to David since their conversation in the restaurant. In fact, he had been avoiding him. Nor had he reported back to Janet as he had promised he would. He couldn't face either of them.

Ponton glanced at the article. There were three photographs at the top of the page. The first two were of Liz Brennan and Vicky Tate. They were head-and-shoulders snapshots, rather blurred as if they had been blown up in size, from passport photos perhaps. The third was different. It showed a tall coloured girl crossing a busy street and shielding her face with her arm. But there was no mistaking who she was. The face that was trying to hide itself from the camera was the face which had stared at Ponton in a shop window in Old Compton Street ten days before. It was the face of Carla Drummond.

He scanned the article rapidly. The gist of it was that the murders remained a mystery and that the police were still pursuing their enquiries, though without any visible sign of success. The new information was at the end. Carla Drummond, a Soho resident who worked as a striptease dancer, had reported being attacked outside her flat. The attacker had been interrupted and Miss Drummond was unharmed. She had been taken to hospital and treated for shock but had not been detained. A boyfriend, who was the only witness, had been slightly injured. A police spokesman had stated that to describe the incident as an attack was a gross exaggeration. There was no reason to suppose that the intruder had intended to do Miss Drummond any harm or that this occurrence was in any way associated with the deaths of two women in recent months – in connection with which, incidentally, a number of highly significant lines of investigation were being pursued at this very moment in time.

Ponton's nerves needed steadying. He went into the kitchen and made himself a second pot of tea, and refilled his pipe. The murders were creeping closer again. The thing that stood out from the page and hit him in the face was the fact that this attack, or whatever it was, had taken place in the evening of the day he had spent in London – the evening David was supposed to have spent in a hotel in Russell Square.

This had all happened over a week ago. It must have been in the

119

papers at the time. Fortunately he had forgotten to put the newspapers in the dustbin that week. He went through the pile and found the one for the day after his trip to London. There was nothing. He tried the next day. There was a tiny article in the bottom corner of an inside page. No wonder he'd missed it. It told him no more than the Sunday article, in fact rather less. By this time Ponton was puffing so furiously on his pipe that sparks flew out of the bowl and nearly set fire to his dressing gown. He was in an agony of frustration. Once again something had happened and he did not have sufficient information to make sense of it. He knew that the attack on Carla was connected with the murders, just as he had known that the blackmail was connected. From the moment he saw the policemen in David's office, from the moment Janet had shown him the letter, he had had a sense of doom, of a black cloud hovering over him and over David, threatening to engulf and suffocate them both.

It was not that he suspected David of any real involvement in the murders. He had not considered that as a possibility for even one minute. Well, not seriously. He did consider him capable of behaving very foolishly in an attempt to get off the hook he had hung himself on. He couldn't help wondering whether David had been stupid enough to pay Carla a nocturnal visit to try to reason with her, or perhaps frighten her. He read through both articles again to see if there was any clue to the attacker's identity. There was none. It was dark and neither Miss Drummond nor her boyfriend had been able to offer any useful description. There was no mention of a motive for the attack, and no mention of blackmail. Carla may have been in shock but she seemed to have kept her mouth shut about that.

He needed more information. Or, if he was going to be sensible about it, he needed to forget the whole wretched business and get back to his own work. He knew that was impossible. As long as the murders remained unsolved, as long as there was the possibility of another murder, he would never have peace of mind again. They had completely disrupted his life, ruined his sleep, and sent him scurrying around London when he had far better things to do. And he did not imagine for one moment that the worst was over yet. If the police declined to solve them – and they did not seem to be in any hurry – then he would simply have to do it himself. It should not be that difficult. After all, Ponton was supposed to be intelligent. A man who was capable of understanding *Aspects of the Theory of Syntax* – in so far as it was intelligible – should be able to make sense of the striptease murders.

His first priority, then, was more information. The sort of stuff the newspapers provided was no use at all. He needed to know everything the police knew, and preferably more besides. The question of where he would obtain such information was no sooner asked than the answer became obvious. There was one person who would know far more about what was happening in Soho than any newspaper. Sylvia.

He couldn't do it. As soon as he thought about her, memories of their last evening came crowding together and shoved themselves forward in his mind. He had written to her a couple of times, but that was when he had nothing to say. A letter was no good now. He would have to phone her and find out what she knew. Besides, letters were safe. There was time to choose one's words carefully, time to decide whether one really wanted to post it, time to prepare oneself for the reply. The telephone was dangerous, with her voice on the other end of the line and no time to think.

He was sure he didn't have her number. That was it. He couldn't phone her because he didn't have her number. He fetched his jacket and looked in his address book. The number was there.

He sat down and stared at it. He got up and went into the hall and looked at the telephone. The telephone squatted on its table at the bottom of the stairs and looked back at him. He went into the kitchen, poured himself another cup of tea, put it down beside his chair and sat down. Then he got up, went into the hall, sat on the bottom step of the stairs and dialled the number. The phone rang for a long time. Perhaps she was out. Then he realized it was only ten o'clock in the morning. She was probably still in bed. He pictured her waking up, reaching for the phone. The picture became rather too detailed and he shook it out of his mind. There was a click and the ringing stopped.

A sleepy voice on the other end of the line.

'Oh,' she said, 'fancy it being you. You're up early.'

'How are you?'

'Fine.'

'Are you alone?' He had no sooner said this than he realized it was not a good way to start. It was a totally idiotic way to start. What he'd meant was whether she was able to talk, or rather . . . he didn't know what he'd meant.

Much giggling on the other end of the line, and a lot of puffing and blowing and squeaking of springs. He imagined her sitting up in bed.

'Course I am. Following instructions, remember?'

Ponton remembered. Her voice sounded comfortable, reassuring, but not quite as he expected. It was the voice of a stranger. He was regretting the call already. There was a long pause while they both tried to think of something to say. Then they both started talking at once.

'Sorry,' she said.

'No, go on.'

'Thanks for your letter. It was ever so interesting. Do they always go on like that?'

'Who?'

'At the university.'

'Oh, yes, I suppose they do.' He had written to her weeks ago and told her about some trivial row in the department because he couldn't think of anything else to say. He could only vaguely remember what it was about. He doubted whether she would have understood it.

'I thought you talked about books all the time.'

'Not all the time.'

'Well,' she said, 'you do live and learn.'

There was another pause and more squeaking of bedsprings and then they both started talking at the same time again.

'There was something ...'

'Are you still there? Oh, sorry ...'

'There was something I wanted to ask you.'

'Yes?'

'I read something in the paper. I don't know whether you know her. Carla, was it?'

'Oh her,' she said. 'I wouldn't take much notice of her.'

Ponton had to be careful here. He had to remember that he was supposed never to have heard of Carla Drummond until that morning when he saw her name in the paper. He knew nothing about the blackmail. The last thing he wanted was Sylvia getting wind of the Redgrove affair. It was enough to know that he had made a complete fool of himself, and to know why.

'The paper said she was attacked.'

'Wishful thinking,' she said, and burst out laughing. Her laughter boomed at him out of the receiver. Suddenly her voice sounded unnatural, metallic. She was probably holding the phone too close. He pictured her sitting up in bed, her arm stretched out across the pillow, her hair loose, the phone tucked under her chin. He wondered if she wore a nightdress. Of course she didn't. 'Hang on, though,' she said. 'There was something fishy about that.'

'Yes?'

'Well, didn't I tell you? It was a couple of months ago, just after we ... after you were here ...' There was a pause. 'She had this money. Fifty pounds. She was showing off about it. Carried it round with her. Showing it to everybody in the clubs.'

'Did she say where she got it?' Ponton was trying to keep his voice steady. This was David's money. The first instalment.

'I'll say she did. Mr X. You remember?'

'The mystery man, yes.' Of course, Ponton thought. It was the obvious explanation. People would want to know where she got the money, and she wasn't going to tell them about David.

'She said Vicky told her. I mean, can you believe that?'

'It seems unlikely,' he said. But she had to tell them something once she'd shown them the money, and they'd already heard of Mr X. He was a ready-made explanation for any mysterious sums of money that turned up. In the meantime, David remained her secret. Vicky was the weak point in her story, but not too weak. People might not believe it, but Vicky was in no position to contradict her.

'Vicky would never have told her,' Sylvia was saying. 'Not in a million years. Not if she'd tried to beat it out of her. Everybody says so.'

'No, I'm sure she wouldn't.' Ponton was on dangerous ground here. 'And this happened just the once, I suppose?'

'Well! Funny you should say that.'

'Really?' She had shrieked at him and he moved the phone a little way from his ear.

'It wasn't just once. It happened again.'

'When?'

'Oh, recently. Couple of weeks ago. Fifty pounds again. I didn't see it this time. She wouldn't show it me. She knew I didn't believe her. Everybody else saw it. Carla's got that money again. Carla's got that money off Mr X again.' This was delivered in a high-pitched squeak and it took him a moment to realize she was mimicking voices. 'Got his name off Vicky. Told her just before she died. They had a fight about it. Makes you sick if you ask me.' The last sentence was shrieked at him in her own voice. Sylvia was exactly the sort of person who shrieks down phones.

'Well,' he said, 'it's all a bit of a mystery.'

'You can say that again. Why are you so interested, anyway?'

'I was just curious.'

'You must have been very curious. You've never phoned me before.'

Valid point, Ponton thought.

'I was worried,' he said.

'What about?' He could hear her shuffling around, changing position in the bed. This time he managed to stifle the image.

'Well, if there'd been another attack ...'

'Oh, don't worry. He hasn't got me yet.'

'Good.'

'Is that what you were worried about?' Her voice was suddenly quieter.

'Sorry?'

'You said you were worried. Were you worried about me?'

There was a pause while it dawned on Ponton what he had just talked himself into. He had been so busy getting information out of her without letting slip anything about David that he hadn't noticed the way the conversation was going. There was absolute silence on the other end of the line while she waited for an answer.

'Yes. Yes, course.'

'Do you ever get up to London these days?' she said casually.

'No. Never. Not when the term's on. Terribly busy. Hardly a minute to think.'

'Oh.' There was another long period of silence while Ponton tried to think of something to say. What he wanted to do was finish the conversation and hang up, but he didn't know how to without giving her the opportunity of making all sorts of arrangements and plans for the future and heaven knows what. It occurred to him that if he just put his finger on one of the little buttons on top of the phone and held it down for a second, she'd think they'd been cut off. Would she, though? Would it cut them off? Would she suspect he'd done it? Would she ring him back? The silence was becoming embarrassing.

'Well, it's been nice ...'

'When do you break up?' she said.

'Sorry?'

'For Christmas. Don't you say that at university, break up?'

'Yes, we do.'

'So when do you break up?'

'Oh, I don't know. In about a month.'

'That would be Boxing Day.' She laughed.

'Would it? Three weeks then.'

'I'm taking a week off about that time. I'm not doing anything special. If you're interested.'

It was now or never. The situation was desperate. He jabbed his finger down on the button and held it there. He felt terribly guilty. He lifted his finger off slowly. He expected to hear the dialling tone. There was silence except for a slight crackle.

'Hello?' she said. 'Are you there? Hello?' She was still there, bawling at him. He wondered if she'd go away if he kept quiet. He decided she wouldn't.

'Yes.'

'What happened?'

'I think we got cut off.'

'Oh, oh well, no harm done.'

'No.'

'Was there anything else you wanted to know?'

'Not really, no.'

'I suppose I'd better be going, then,' she said. 'This must be costing you a fortune.'

'Oh, really? All right, then.'

'I might see you?'

'Yes, why not.' Now that it was over and she was nearly gone, he had a ridiculous urge to prolong the conversation. 'I'm sorry if I woke you up.'

'That's all right. Time I was up anyway.'

'I'll be in touch.'

'All my love,' she said. There was an extremely peculiar noise down the phone and it took him a moment to realize that she had blown him a kiss.

'Yes,' he said. 'Thank you.'

He went back into the living room, sat down and had a sip of his tea. It had gone cold.

The rest of the day was a disaster. That night he dreamed of Sylvia. She took all her clothes off, stood in front of him stark naked and demanded that he provide her with a satisfactory definition of a morphophoneme.

Eighteen

Eric waited for a break in the traffic along Oxford Street, crossed over and took one of the roads leading into Cavendish Square. He walked round the square and out at the north end and past a long terrace of large, drab Victorian houses. A bitter wind blew in his face and he dug his fists deep down into the pockets of his overcoat and hunched his shoulders against the cold.

He reached the house and pressed the bell. After a second or two there was a metallic whirring from inside and the door unlocked itself. He pushed it open and went in. The girl was sitting behind her desk as usual, with her head down. He stood with his hands in his pockets and grinned at her. She looked up and saw him and, as always, there was the sudden, startled widening of the eyes, the momentary expression of pleasure or fear. She nodded and looked down again, pretending to sort through a pile of letters on the desk. Eric stood for a while staring at the top of her head, trying to make her look up at him. Then he turned and went into the waiting room. The girl fancied him, though she was working overtime at not showing it. He could always tell.

For once he didn't have long to wait. The old man was working his way through the loonies as per schedule. The girl poked her head round the door, called Eric's name and retreated to the safety of her desk. When he went past her, she was sitting with her head down and still fiddling with her letters. There seemed to be about half a dozen doctors in the house. He didn't know whether they were all shrinks. They popped up from time to time, sticking their heads round the waiting room door to see who was there. Eric's shrink had a little room at the back of the house, at the end of a long corridor. He went past the desk, looking back at the girl over his shoulder, down the corridor

126

and knocked on the door before going in.

The old boy was farting about inside, getting his props ready. He pulled the curtains and straightened the little silver ornament on the window-sill, then smiled at Eric, said something about the weather and asked him if he was warm enough. Eric nodded and took his overcoat off. There was a gas fire on in the corner. The old man smiled again, sat down at his desk and picked up the fountain pen that he always played with while he was putting Eric into hypnosis. Eric sat down in the chair, made himself comfortable, dropped his arms by his sides and let his hands flop loosely on to his knees. He knew the routine. The man swivelled his chair round so that he was facing Eric across the corner of his desk and asked him if he was ready. Eric nodded again. He had hated the old man on sight, but he had also decided that he was going to be pretty easy to deal with. He reminded him of his uncle Ponton.

Actually, these sessions had become quite an agreeable part of Eric's week. He'd been a bit apprehensive at first, afraid the old man might find things out. He needn't have worried. All the man wanted was for him to talk. Eric talked. Some of it was true and some of it wasn't. He mixed it up. Just enough truth to be plausible. He knew the difference. He'd been confused about that at one time. He'd imagined he'd done things when he hadn't done them. He'd even imagined he'd killed Vicky. He knew that wasn't possible. He was straight about that now. He was straight about a lot of things.

So Eric talked and the old man smiled and made notes with his fountain pen on little coloured sheets of paper and said yes, yes. The only thing he ever said while Eric was talking was yes. Yes ... yes ... yes. Eric's story-telling became more and more imaginative, but all he ever said was yes. Rule one in the shrink's handbook. Never react. Never sound as if you're shocked.

The hypnosis was under way. Eric concentrated on the little silver ornament on the window-sill, then closed his eyes and began to breathe deeply. The man began talking to him, slowly, rhythmically, in time with his breathing. He was supposed to be imagining something beautiful, picturing a beautiful place, a beach or a forest, where he felt calm and happy. He couldn't. There was no such place. He didn't find places beautiful. They were interesting or boring but never beautiful. He didn't know what it meant. Instead he thought of Vicky, and the way she used to look at him in the clubs when he'd been staring at her face –

127

that wonderful look of pure hate.

The old man had got on to the relaxation stuff. Eric was supposed to think about each part of his body, from his feet up through his legs, arms, stomach, back, chest, shoulders, up to his neck and jaws. He had to feel them relaxing one by one. He went along with it, shuffling his feet about, repositioning his hands on his knees, letting his shoulders droop. He realized how tightly his jaw was clenched and let it sag. There was no danger in any of this. He knew he didn't lose control. The old man thought he did, but Eric had been fooling him. Behind his closed eyes there was no beautiful place. There was only Vicky.

She was dancing. He was sitting in the dark, and in front of him on a brightly-lit stage Vicky was dancing for him. Her face was blank, expressionless, her gaze fixed somewhere above and behind him. Her arms hung at her sides. Only her legs were moving, weaving patterns across the stage, faster and faster. The lights revolved – red, blue, silver – the music played and Vicky danced. Eric watched her face, never taking his eyes off her, waiting. The music stopped and she fell to her knees in a circle of light, but still she didn't look at him. It started again, slower, quieter. She lowered herself gently and lay on her side. For a moment she looked down. He leaned forward in his seat and their eyes met.

It was not faked, not like the others. The others pretended, but with Vicky it was always real. If his eyes caught hers, there was nothing she could do to stop the hate flowing out. And it was all his. There was no one else in the room. There was only him and Vicky and the bond between them. He ignored the others. He despised them, with their tricks and their games. He had waited patiently for perfection and it had been given to him in Vicky. Given and then taken away. He knew that he could never have hurt her. He could never have killed her. But he knew who had.

The man was counting. He counted from one to five and when he reached five Eric was supposed to wake up. It seemed only a moment or two since he had closed his eyes, but it must have been longer. Three, four, five. Eric blinked a couple of times, opened his eyes and looked across the room. The old man was smiling at him.

128

Nineteen

It was on a cold bright morning in the first week of December that Inspector Wright had occasion to call on Mr Monty Snow at home. Monty had phoned Vine Street the evening before and said that he had information which he wished to impart to the police. As soon as the inspector got to the office that morning, he had called the Snow White. He was informed by the ponce on the other end of the line that Monty had been struck down with flu and was at home for the day. He phoned the unlisted number and talked to Monty who, admittedly, had sounded a bit under the weather. Would it be convenient if the inspector called on him at home? No, it most emphatically would not. His information, which he would not discuss over the phone, would keep until he was back at work. Monty further suggested that if police investigations were proceeding at their normal pace, a day or two was neither here nor there. The inspector had said that he entirely understood the delicacy of the situation, thanked Mr Snow for his co-operation, and promptly found out the address and set off. Policeman's prerogative.

He decided to go by train. Monty lived about an hour out of Waterloo on the Bournemouth line. He could have driven down but he preferred the train. The inspector liked trains. He'd done a bit of spotting in his youth and still took an interest when he had the chance. Well, to be honest, it had been quite a passion at one time. He'd even dreamed, when he was a boy, of making a career of it. He still remembered the day when he'd discovered that train-spotting was not a possible profession. It wasn't the same now, of course, with all this electric stuff. The inspector was a steam man. Those were the days to be a policeman, chasing round the country in steam trains and big black squad cars. Now it was all pandas, and superintendents buggering off to Europe in aeroplanes.

The inspector looked around appreciatively at the hustle and bustle of Waterloo. It was all tarted up now, but there was still something about railway stations that took him straight back to his childhood, back to the little boy in short trousers standing on the platform with his pencil and notebook and his engine spotter's guide. He took his time locating the Bournemouth train and settling himself into his carriage. He looked nostalgically at the grime on the windows, took his glasses off and cleaned them, and lit a pipe.

The inspector did not entertain high hopes for Monty's information, but they couldn't afford to overlook anything. That was the way they did it. Look at everything, masses of detail, look for a pattern. Bit like train-spotting. He wondered if that was why he enjoyed it. Well, sometimes he enjoyed it. He wasn't getting a lot of joy out of the present case. Nobody was. Officially they were following a number of leads. Unofficially they were stuck. The newspapers had been giving them hell, especially since a tart called Drummond had come up with a story about ghostly fingers up and down her spine while her boyfriend was out getting the booze in. Personally, the inspector was of the opinion that she'd already had a few before the event. She'd had police protection for a few days but, manpower being what it was, they couldn't afford even one constable hanging round strip clubs all day and waiting for something to go bump in the night. Besides, this Drummond already had the full-time services of the said boyfriend – large black party, built like a brick shithouse, name of Thomas.

The infuriating thing was that it was a relatively straightforward case. Two strippers murdered. Modus operandi consistent, therefore same party responsible. Said party known to the victims. Silly bitches opened the door and let him in. Fingerprints were no help. The Brennan woman had had open house the night before and half the tarts in Soho had been in there poking about, plus Eric Wells and assorted ponces from the vicinity. Same story with the Tate woman. Her own prints all over the place, young Eric again who'd dropped by for a sniff at her underwear, Monty who'd done the necessary with the front door, and Sylvia Mothersill's prints all over the kitchen where she seemed to have made herself at home, and on the telephone where she'd finally got around to notifying the police.

130

All the suspects who were visible had been accounted for.

Eric Wells. Raving psychopath if the inspector had ever seen one. Walking advert for euthanasia. Definitely in Southampton for the Tate murder. Alibi like the rock of Gibraltar.

The old professor, Ponton. Peculiar taste in overweight strippers, but hardly the type. Nowhere near London for Liz Brennan's murder.

Another professor, Redgrove. Taste for skinny strippers. Another alibi. Amazing what went on in these universities. Not a lot to do with education, if you cared to ask the inspector's opinion.

Monty himself. Knew the victims. Had a row with both of them at some time or another, in the line of business. Not very likely to go berserk at his time of life, though you never could tell.

Then there was Mr Smith, the lemon sweet merchant. They hadn't quite succeeded in laying hands on him yet. Gone to earth. Hadn't been near a strip club for months. Hardly promising material for a murderer. None of them were.

The official version, of course, for the consumption of the press and anyone else who might care to ask, was the nutter story. Down from Cleethorpes for the day, quick bit of business in Soho, back home for supper and feet up in front of the telly. No need to tell everybody which way your enquiries were going. Besides, it sounded a lot better to announce that you were scouring the whole of Britain for a maniac and hadn't quite managed to come up with one yet than to admit you were only looking round the square mile of Soho. Anyway, they would see what Brother Monty had to say for himself.

The inspector had now arrived at his destination. He made enquiries and set off to walk the half-mile or so from the station to the Snow residence. It was less than forty miles from the centre of London but it could have been a different planet. Typical English country town. All tweeds and headscarves and silly buggers on horseback. He walked through the town centre – it was just a crossroads with a few shops – and out on a long, winding road that led into the countryside. He arrived at Monty's front door. And very nice too. So this was where he escaped to after the rigours of the working day. No wonder he didn't want police enquiries extending to this little retreat.

It was a large detached house standing back from the road in a nice bit of garden, four-bedroom, possibly five, roses round the door, ivy creeping all over the place, garage like an aircraft hangar, you name it. The inspector took it all in. You could bet he didn't have a mortgage. Not in his business. He rang the bell and wondered if it would be opened by the butler. It was opened by Monty, very nattily attired in cardigan and slacks, cravat round his neck – the inspector hadn't seen one of those in a few years – and a look of gratifying consternation across his bruiser's countenance.

'Morning,' the inspector said, looking up at the sky. It was clear, pale blue, crossed with thin lines of cloud like aeroplane trails. 'Turned out nice.'

Monty said something that sounded like 'bordig', scrabbled in the pocket of his cardigan, fetched out a handkerchief and blew his nose loudly.

'You don't sound too well.' Monty just stood there, looking at him and fidgeting with his hankie. 'Could I have a word, if it's convenient?'

'Won't it keep?' Monty said.

'I shouldn't think so, no.' The inspector smiled affably and put his foot in the door.

Monty looked as if he might be considering the consequences of slamming it in his face, then turned and walked back down the hall, leaving the inspector to close the door. Monty had disappeared inside and the inspector heard voices. He had a look around, taking in the grandfather clock, the long curve of polished banister, the brass stair rods, the pictures on the wall. And a very respectable class of picture it was too. None of your filth. None of your erotica. His visit was obviously a cause of embarrassment, which gave him a quiet satisfaction. He found out why when he got into the living room. Monty was entertaining a lady to morning tea. A table was set with cups and jugs and teapot, and a bright-eyed old bird of about Monty's age with too much make-up was watching the inspector with obvious curiosity.

Monty did the introductions with a marked reluctance and the inspector made himself comfortable in an armchair. Mrs Willoughby. The inspector was delighted to make her acquaintance. Mrs Willoughby was charmed. Monty was squirming with embarrassment and blowing his nose at two-minute intervals. Polite conversation followed and the inspector asked an innocent question or two. Widow. Lived up the road. Bit of money put by, no doubt. He had done some checking up on Monty. Lived alone. No record of matrimony. His policeman's mind put two and two together. At Mrs W's suggestion, Monty went into the kitchen to fetch another cup. The inspector helped himself to a fairy cake.

'I hope it's nothing serious,' Mrs Willoughby said confidentially when Monty had disappeared and could be heard blowing his nose explosively in the kitchen.

'Oh no, madam.' The inspector balanced the cake between a hairy thumb and forefinger and examined it forensically before taking a bite. 'Traffic accident. Mr Snow was a witness.'

'Really? Well, I'm sure he'd be a very reliable one. You have to be in his business.'

'I don't think I caught Mr Snow's line of business,' he said casually, flicking a crumb off his jacket.

'He's in insurance. He works on the floor, you know.'

'On the floor?'

'At Lloyd's.'

'Oh, I see.'

'It's a great privilege. It takes them years to get on the floor.'

'Yes, I'm sure it does.'

'That's why he wears that funny black suit. They all do. It's tradition. He looks quite different when he takes it off.'

'I suppose he would.'

Preceded by a tremendous sneeze, Monty returned with the cup.

'You naughty man,' Mrs Willoughby said.

There was a horrible pause. Monty swayed slightly. The inspector gave him a pleasant smile and took out his pipe.

'Sorry?' Monty said.

'You didn't tell me you'd seen an accident.'

'Accident?' Monty glanced at the inspector and tried to get his bearings.

'The one you witnessed,' the inspector said helpfully.

'Oh that one. Yes. Terrible. Blood all over the place.'

Mrs Willoughby tut-tutted.

'He doesn't like to tell me things that might upset me,' she told the inspector.

'I can see that.'

The conversation flagged. The inspector drank his tea. Monty didn't seem very talkative at all. The inspector lit his pipe, with Mrs Willoughby's permission, and smiled at everybody. He was enjoying this.

'Well,' the lady said, 'I'd better leave you boys to it, if it's official business.' Monty received his kiss on the cheek with a certain lack of enthusiasm, the inspector thought. 'Now you will look after yourself. And don't go back to work until you're better. They can manage without you. Isn't that right, inspector?'

'Absolutely.'

Monty helped her on with her coat.

'Now you be a good boy. Promise.'

Monty promised.

'Very agreeable party,' the inspector said with a nod towards the door when Mrs Willoughby had left. Might as well rub it in before they got down to business. 'Known her long?'

'Who? Mrs W?' You'd have thought half a dozen women had been round kissing him on the cheek. 'No, not long. Few months. Neighbour.'

'Very agreeable.'

'Couldn't it have waited?'

'Sorry?' The inspector looked bewildered.

'I said couldn't it have waited? Until I was at the club. Instead of coming round here. Invading my privacy.'

'Ah well, that's for me to decide, isn't it? It might be important. It might be just the thing we've been waiting for. We might have to act on it immediately. You never know.' Monty didn't look convinced. 'Well, come on, let's have it.'

'Mr X.' Monty poured himself another cup of tea. 'Heard of him?'

The inspector's heart sank. He had heard of Mr X. The whole of Soho had heard of him. The newspapers had heard of him. Cash had been offered to anybody who could name him. Half the women in England had rung up and denounced every man in the family down to their grandfathers. The inspector didn't believe a word of it. Liz Brennan had been on the game in her day. Probably reverted to type, earned herself fifty quid and made up a long story to cover it up. He had seen a few red herrings in his time, but this one was a classic.

'Go on,' he said.

'Well, Liz and Vicky got that money out of him, right? Then they're dead so nobody knows who he is. Then Carla knows who he is. Then she gets money off him.'

'Hang about.' The inspector had perked up considerably and had taken his notebook out. 'Who's this Carla? Carla Drummond?'

134

'That's it.'

'How did she get his name?'

'Off Vicky. Before she died. They had a row, Carla and Vicky. Must have been quite a fight. Anyway, she got the name off her. Now one theory ...'

'Skip the theory. Did you witness this fight?'

'No, I heard about it. Everybody heard about it.'

'Who from?'

Monty thought for a while.

'Carla.'

'Did you see the money?'

'Course I did. Everybody saw it.' Monty was here convulsed in a sneezing fit. He blew his nose and recovered himself. 'It was fifty in tens. She was flashing it about. Everybody had a look.'

'When was this?'

'The first time?'

'How many bloody times were there?'

'Two.'

'All right, the first time.'

'Well, it must have been, oh, a couple of months ago. She had this money in an envelope. Said she'd got the name off Vicky and he'd paid up.'

'And you didn't feel like mentioning this to us at the time?'

'I didn't think it was important.' The inspector felt that Monty's splutterings into his hankie were less than convincing at this point. 'Anyway, I thought you'd hear about it. Then there was that business with somebody trying to kill her. Well I know nothing happened, but she reckons he was trying to kill her. Well, it changes things, doesn't it? I mean, if somebody's really after her, it changes things. I thought you ought to know.'

'All right, all right, we'll come back to that point.' The inspector scribbled ominously in his notebook. 'Second time. When?'

'Month ago.'

'Go on.'

'Same thing. Fifty in tens. Then Thomas gets hold of her.'

'Boyfriend? Big black effort?'

'That's him. Gets hold of her, tells her to shut up, grabs the money and stuffs it in his pocket. They had a fight about it, right in the middle of the club. Dreadful language,' Monty said. 'Then he hits her.'

'You saw all this?'

135

'Yes.'

'Go on.'

'That's about it. The way I see it ...' Monty began, and the inspector held up his hand. He was not interested in the way Monty saw it. Nor was he interested in Mr X. He didn't believe that story now any more than he had done ten minutes ago. If ▸ Carla Drummond knew his identity, why hadn't she called the police and demanded the reward like the rest of the population? Why risk blackmail for fifty quid when she could earn a great deal more quite legally with a phone call? No, what interested the inspector was that Drummond and Thomas what's-his-face were blackmailing somebody, possibly in connection with the murders.

'Now,' he said, 'I'll tell you what we're going to do. We're going to sit here and have a nice cup of tea and you're going to tell me the whole thing again, slowly, step by step, detail by detail, and we're going to keep on until I'm satisfied that I know everything you know. And I don't care if it takes all day. Is that clear?'

'I suppose so.'

When the inspector was finally satisfied, he closed his notebook. He didn't stay much longer at Monty's after that. If there was one thing he disliked, it was being told things he didn't know and should have known. And if there was another, it was being told them by cocky porn-merchants with detached houses in Surrey and no mortgage. As soon as he got back to the railway station, he made a phone call to London.

Thomas – the object of the inspector's call – had spent the last hour innocently drinking his lunch in his favourite pub in Charing Cross Road. Sylvia came in for a quick break between spots and he offered to buy her a drink. It proved more expensive than he'd expected because she'd spotted a large slab of bacon and egg pie, but he felt like company, somebody other than Carla, and he'd always liked Sylvia.

Carla had been driving him round the twist ever since the business at the flat. He still didn't know what had happened except that somebody had come down the stairs at him like a bat out of hell, knocked him flying and written off the best part of a crate of light ale. Apparently he had been lurking in the corridor and jumped out on her when she came out of the flat. She'd been hysterical for a week. They'd had the police round asking questions about Thomas's business affairs, which was highly undesirable, the press round taking photos and all sorts of people hanging about outside and staring up at the windows for hours on end. Thomas was a man who appreciated his privacy.

The only good thing to come out of it was that Carla's mouth seemed to have been shut permanently on the subject of Redgrove. Thomas had been furious about that. She had nearly blown the whole thing. The agreement was that the money was to be spent quietly, little by little, and she was to tell him the moment she had Redgrove on the hook. He'd found out about the first instalment from one of the girls at Monty's. She'd no sooner got her hands on the money than she'd done the rounds of the clubs, waving it under the noses of all the girls and anybody else who happened to be around. He had hit her for that. Which hadn't stopped her from doing exactly the same thing a month later. The attack had changed all that. She was terrified. He'd been afraid she'd blurt everything out to the police, but she hadn't said a word.

The other thing that was getting on his nerves was that he was now in the business of permanent bodyguard. She wouldn't go anywhere without him. He had to take her to work in the morning, escort her between clubs and bring her home at night. It was doing nothing for his social calendar. But since she was the wage-earner he didn't really have too much room for complaint. Thomas had never adapted well to employment. She'd wanted to give up the clubs altogether but he had soon put a stop to that idea.

'How's she feeling now, then?' Sylvia said. She polished off the last of the pie and wiped her fingers on a kleenex. 'She seems more cheerful.'

He had been telling her about his troubles, or some of them.

'Still making a hell of a fuss.'

'I'm not surprised. I'd be making a fuss if it'd been me.'

'I don't think he was up to anything. He hardly touched her. Probably somebody who'd lost his way.'

'Where? Up the end of your corridor? Where was he going? It's not exactly the high street.'

'Suppose not.' To be honest, at the time the incident had frightened him more than he'd admitted, though he'd quickly decided there was nothing in it. Carla was more to him than just a source of income. They'd been together a long time.

'So you don't think it was him?'

'Who?'

137

'HIM!' she said, 'Jack the Ripper.'

'Doubt it. He's not after blacks. He likes them white and juicy. More like you.'

'Y'bugger,' she said, and punched him on the shoulder. 'Look, I really have to be off. I've got a spot five minutes ago. Can't keep the public waiting.' She finished her drink, wiped the crumbs off her lips and heaved herself off the bar stool. 'Thanks for the drink.'

'Pleasure,' he said. 'I'll walk you down the road.'

They came out of the pub and straight into the arms of two policemen who were waiting outside. They were looking for Thomas. Would he mind accompanying them to the station and assisting them a little further in their enquiries?

'What's it about?' he said.

'Just a couple of questions.'

There were actually three of them. One was standing in front of him, one behind, and the third one was sitting in a car which was parked up on the kerb, holding the door open. Thomas did not feel he could refuse.

Sylvia stood and watched them drive away, then she turned round and saw Eric. He was standing on the corner looking at her in that funny way of his. She thought of going and saying something to him but she didn't have time. She waved.

On her way to her next spot at Monty's, she made up her mind about what she would have to do that evening. It was this decision which would lead, in the early hours of the following morning, to the end of the affair of the Striptease Murders.

Twenty

At about the time that Thomas was receiving his invitation to Vine Street, Ponton was sitting in the university staffroom in Southampton trying to read the newspaper and becoming increasingly annoyed by a very loud conversation behind him. He had had his lunch and, on sticking his head round the staffroom door and finding it empty for once, he settled down in an armchair to pass the time until his two o'clock lecture. He had just about finished the front page when the professor of theology arrived accompanied by one of his acolytes, and they had begun a noisy dissection of a PhD thesis which had been submitted to them. Ponton put up with it for a while, then made a great fuss of folding up his newspaper, getting up, carrying it to the far side of the room, sitting down and opening it again. The conversation became, if anything, rather louder. Divine matters took precedence, presumably, over the reading of newspapers.

'It's not that it's a bad argument as such,' the professor was saying. 'It's just not strong enough for the theoretical weight that's being hung on it.'

The acolyte agreed at sufficient length to indicate that he knew what the professor was on about.

Bang goes three years' work for some poor devil, Ponton thought. He put his paper down and got up and walked out.

He spent half an hour wandering round the campus in rather a daze. That last scrap of conversation had had the most peculiar effect on him. At first he thought he had heard it before. Then he had the idea that it reminded him of something somebody had once said to him. Somebody had told him about something not being strong enough. He was sure it was important that he should remember, but he just couldn't place it. It was still bothering him as he made his way across to the lecture theatre where his first-year undergraduates were waiting for him. He was giving them a brief trot through phonological theory from Trubetzkoy to Halle, complete with diagrams. The diagrams didn't make a lot of sense, but they weren't to know. It was the sort of thing he could do in his sleep, which was a good job because his mind was elsewhere.

He was halfway through Roman Jakobson when the penny dropped and he remembered what he'd been told. The rest of the lecture was rather garbled and it ended ten minutes early, which won him a round of applause from the undergraduates, who probably hadn't had their lunch. He had no more classes for the day, and he went home in a state of extreme agitation such as generally occurred when he had read a book which did him the discourtesy of presenting him with an argument that didn't work. The thing he'd remembered had thrown a completely new light on the murders. All sorts of possibilities were opening up and he needed to think them through.

Sylvia was having a bad day. Monty had started his Xmas Special – the first week in December, mind you – and she was one of Santa's presents. This involved her spending the first five minutes of her act inside a sack. It was too tight and very rough and when she wriggled about in it, as she was supposed to do, it rubbed against her skin and gave her a rash. There were also bits that came off the inside of it and got up her nose. So she emerged red raw and sneezing, which probably wasn't very sexy. Not that she cared. Another hazard of the sack was that she always wanted to pee the moment she got into the bloody thing, and at ten-minute intervals from then on. It must be psychological.

The other thing that was bothering her was seeing Thomas being carted off by the police. She didn't know what it was about, but she could guess it had something to do with the money. She wondered if Carla knew. She hadn't seen her all day. She could imagine the state she would be in if Thomas wasn't there to pick her up and she didn't know where he was. Sylvia had decided, when she saw Thomas being taken away, that she would offer to walk Carla back to her flat when they finished work that evening and stay there with her if she wanted. She'd never liked Carla but she was one of the gang, and if you can't do somebody a favour

140

when they're in trouble what's life all about? Sylvia was on at the Reveille later and she would see if Carla was there.

Ponton, meanwhile, had spent the first part of the afternoon going round the house talking to himself and tidying everything in sight. This consisted of picking up any movable object in his path, examining it, flicking at it with his handkerchief and putting it back in exactly the same place. He did rearrange a few books on the shelves, but this was particularly pointless since he knew he would move them back again. At frequent intervals his pipe refused to function under the demands imposed on it and had to be poked and prodded at both ends with pipe-cleaners, matches and anything else that came to hand.

All this was a necessary part of the process of serious thought, but he finally sat down and forced himself to read through the notes which he had made with Sylvia on that memorable night in Highgate. He hadn't looked at them since then. He had put them in a drawer as soon as he got back from London and then managed to convince himself that he'd lost them. This was his usual procedure with things he didn't want to read, such as highly significant modern novels which any literate person was obliged to be familiar with. But this time he'd gone too far. In an excess of enthusiasm to demonstrate to himself that he had in fact lost them, he had opened the drawer one day and there they were. He put them on the table beside his armchair, where they had remained ever since.

His main fear as far as the notes were concerned was of the memories they might awake, the things that might be called to mind. He was right. He no sooner began flicking through the pages of the note-pad than Sylvia was sitting opposite him in the other armchair with a glass of brandy in her hand and her toes tucked down the side of the cushion. He exorcized Sylvia, with some difficulty, and began reading the notes through slowly and carefully from the beginning. This was the laborious part of the process, the checking of details. He found a pen and sat scribbling more notes on top of the ones he'd already made. A completely new story began to take shape. The pile of used match-sticks mounted up in the ashtray beside his chair.

As with the development of all theories, there were two stages. First there was the idea, the impetus – in this case a random event

141

which creates the inspiration so that old facts can be linked together in a new way. This had started with the conversation in the staffroom, which he would never have heard if he had decided to take his lunch half an hour earlier. Suddenly everything had changed, and everything he thought he knew about the murders had to be looked at again in the light of the new discovery. Once he had seen the flaw in the argument, he couldn't understand how he'd missed it before. Well, yes he could. He'd been talked into missing it. Everyone had made an axiomatic assumption for which there was no justification, and he had simply gone along with it. He had to start again at the beginning, making new connections, linking the known events together to make a new pattern. This was what he was doing while he appeared to be engaged in a frantic bout of tidying up.

He had now moved on to the second stage, the checking of facts. The little piece of the jigsaw which had suddenly slipped into place while he was rabbiting on about Jakobson related to the second murder, Vicky's murder, so he concentrated on that first. He looked closely at the movements of everyone involved. Then there was the hammock, the mysterious man in the doorway, and the even more mysterious case of a telephone which was engaged when there was only supposed to be a dead body in the room. Some of the problems, he decided, resulted from accidents and some from deliberate lies, and he had to separate them out. It took him a long time to get an idea about the telephone, and then he wasn't sure. But it was all making sense for the first time.

He worked back from Vicky's death to Liz Brennan's, the first link in the chain. There wasn't a great deal here that needed checking. It was mainly a question of understanding a state of mind. Ideally, he needed one more piece of information that wasn't available. He needed to know what had been said at the party on the night before Liz died. Sylvia had told him about it in general terms, but he needed to know exactly. Without it, the motivation was a problem, though perhaps not a serious one. He had realized by this point that he was dealing with a madman.

He'd been trying very hard not to think of it in that way, in terms of people or consequences. He had managed to work it out by treating it as a puzzle, an academic exercise. He had sat smoking his pipe and thinking through all the ins and outs of the problem, moving people around like the pieces of a jigsaw, trying them in different places to see whether they would fit. It was a

142

purely intellectual problem, purely a matter of logic. Change one of the premises and the whole chain of inferences changes. He tried to keep this up for as long as he could, fussing about over details, telling himself that he hadn't fully understood it yet. But he knew that sooner or later he would have to make a decision. He would have to do something unless he wanted to wake up one morning and read in the newspaper about the third murder, the one he could have prevented.

He had to face the fact that someone he knew, someone he had sat and talked to, was capable of murder, had committed murder, and was planning to commit another. For if there was one conclusion which was inescapable it was that Carla Drummond was in mortal danger. There had been one attempt on her life and there would be another. She would die without ever knowing what she had done to bring such retribution upon her. The only sensible thing to do, of course, was to get in touch with the police and tell them everything he knew. But that wasn't really an option whether he was right or wrong. Especially if he was right. He was pretty sure he was.

He knew he had to do something. He went out into the hall and sat on the stairs and dialled a number. The phone rang unanswered at the other end. He looked at his watch. Of course it did. Without giving himself time to change his mind, he dialled again. This time he rang the station and asked about train times to London. Carla Drummond had to be warned. If he wasn't prepared to go to the police then he would have to do it himself, and it had to be done as soon as possible.

Sylvia had now arrived at the Reveille, where they hadn't heard about Christmas yet and she had a blessed release from the horrors of Santa's sack. There was no sign of Carla here either, and none of the girls knew where she was. She might come in in the evening, or there were half a dozen other clubs where she might be. Sylvia didn't fancy finishing work at midnight and then traipsing round all of them, and they'd probably miss each other anyway. The best thing would be to go straight to Carla's flat when she'd finished her last spot and see if she was there. Not that she expected any thanks for it.

It was dusk when Ponton left the house. He had decided to walk to the station to give himself more time to think, or perhaps time to change his mind. He took his gloves out of his overcoat pockets and pulled them on as he walked, and suddenly realized he hadn't brought anything with him in case he needed to spend the night. He had no idea how long he would be away, how long it would take. He didn't even have an umbrella. He wondered if he should go back and pack a few things. But going back was dangerous. Once he was back in his own house, he might not feel like coming out again. He walked on.

There were no colours at this time of the evening, only shades of grey. Grey houses, grey trees. An orange street light on an invisible pole burst into life and hovered against the sky like a distant spaceship. As he walked past the houses, he found himself peering into people's living rooms wherever there was a light on, hoping to see someone inside, hoping for company. He wanted reassurance that there were ordinary people inside doing ordinary things like making the dinner and putting the children to bed, and that his mission was an aberration, a disturbance in the natural order of things which would soon be corrected.

What he really wanted was to turn round and go home and pretend that none of it was happening. Pretend he had never overheard the conversation in the staffroom. Pretend he had never read the notes. Pretend that he wasn't really on his way to London to confront a murderer.

Twenty-one

Ponton arrived in London in one of the foulest moods he had enjoyed for a long time. He hated being away from his own fireside in the evenings and he hated not knowing where he was going to spend the night. He couldn't remember for sure whether he'd locked up properly and he was convinced he would get back home to find the place burgled.

For the last hour of the journey he had seen nothing of the world outside his carriage except the lights of the occasional station flashing past. The windows had become mirrors, and when he tried to look out he saw his own reflection looking back at him. He also hated not knowing where he was. He pressed his nose against the window and cupped his hands round his face each time a station went past, but he still couldn't see anything. He huddled back in his seat, put his feet up and went through the whole wretched business again in his mind for the umpteenth time, becoming more and more certain that he was right and wishing more and more that he had never come. When he stepped off on to the platform at Waterloo and the cold air hit him in the face, he felt light-headed and rather queasy as if he were drunk.

Waterloo was its usual hideous self, with half the people rushing about like a speeded-up film and the other half standing round in little groups and staring gormlessly up at the departure boards as if awaiting a sign from heaven. Music, involving trumpets but not otherwise celestial, played above their heads and they were rewarded from time to time with an unearthly voice communicating its message in a secret language. He stood and looked around him, taking in the bustling, glittering, manic awfulness of London at night.

There was something sinister about all these people rushing past him with their faces frozen into masks, or chattering like monkeys. For a moment he had the sensation that he had stumbled into some other world which only came into being as the sun went down and whose inhabitants had no existence during the day. The other day-people knew how to avoid it, but no one had told him and he had somehow wandered into it and become trapped. He was the only human being there, and these were creatures of some other sort who were pushing him slowly and seemingly by accident towards the mouth of one of the tunnels that led into the underground. He knew he was being paranoid, but under the circumstances this seemed an entirely reasonable thing to be.

Ponton descended the escalator, bought his ticket and found his platform. He tried to light a pipe but there was a gale blowing down there and his matches kept going out. The train arrived. He minded the gap, sat down and spent the journey playing his paranoia game with his fellow-passengers. Perhaps they were only pretending to be unaware of him. Perhaps they were all conspirators and the whole scene was being enacted for his benefit, to reassure him that everything was normal as he was carried through the tunnels into the heart of London.

At Piccadilly he came up out of the electric glare of the underground into the twinkling lights of the West End. It glittered like some enormous Christmas tree. Thank God he hadn't seen one of those yet. He walked through the crowds towards Leicester Square and turned into Soho. The worst thing about it all was the lights. There was no natural light and no natural colour. There were green lights, blue lights, red, yellow, lights from cars, from shops, street lights, luminous traffic signs. The real world was shut out as completely as it had been by the windows of the railway carriage. The most beautiful stained glass was outshone by a hundred yards of any Soho street. The effect was eerie. It gave colour where there was none – the pavements glistened yellow – and took it away from where it should have been. The faces of the people were a uniform grey which modulated from time to time into the colours of whatever illumination they were passing. They were more lavishly and eccentrically dressed than the people at Waterloo, but it did not make them any more real. They were flat and indistinct like wandering ghosts, their colours borrowed from their surroundings.

He walked around aimlessly for a while, trying to work up the enthusiasm to start looking for Carla Drummond. Eventually he went to the Reveille and asked for her. They had not seen her. They sent him to Monty's. She wasn't there either. He spent what seemed like hours trailing round clubs and being made to feel utterly ridiculous, like some love-sick admirer hanging round the stage door. In some places he was received politely and in others he was not. People looked him up and down and called upon others to look him up and down. He was advised to forget it and go home and play with himself instead. He was threatened with physical violence and with the police. More sympathetically, he was offered various memorable alternatives if Carla were not to be found. It was with considerable relief that he finally tracked her down to a dingy club in a back alley off Wardour Street.

Unlike Monty's, this club was on two levels. There was a tiny foyer at street level where he paid his money – it was a pound more expensive than Monty's and they dispensed with the formality of filling in a card – and then he descended two twisting staircases to reach a larger room where, as the man at the door had informed him, a very dirty show was in progress. He was very conscious of being underground. He tried to work out whether he was still under the foyer of the club or somewhere under the streets of Soho with people walking about above his head. Either way, he was cozily buried under the earth where the cold of the overground world couldn't reach. There was nothing he could do until Carla had performed, and then the next part of the plan could be put into effect. He was rather apprehensive about being underground. He felt trapped. But he was glad of the delay, and the warmth.

Actually, the man at the door was wrong. The show was much the same as the one he had seen at Monty's but the atmosphere was different at night, or perhaps it was just that he knew what to expect. There seemed to be a bond between the girls and the old men which he had not noticed before. They were obviously trying their best, the men applauded at the end of each act, and the girls acknowledged the applause with a nod of the head. Ponton had been standing in the aisle near the door, ready for escape, but he quickly gave that up and found an empty seat. He had lit a pipe and didn't even remember doing it. He did notice that the man in front of him was very tall and had an extremely large head, and he had to twist about in his seat to see what was going on.

The girls sitting naked on the stage were almost close enough to touch, but untouchable. They were friendly and reassuring though no more real than the people outside, with the colours of their

147

flesh blanched out by the lights. A girl who reminded him a little of Sylvia had recognized a regular customer in the front row and she chatted and joked with him, quite unself-consciously, as she carried on with her stripping. One girl had got the giggles halfway through her act and another girl poked her head round the curtain at the side of the stage and tried to make her laugh. The girl on stage turned and looked at the one behind the curtain, and for a moment it was as if they were alone and the men did not exist. Ponton wondered what it was like backstage, and had a sudden insight into a strange, alien world of female companionship. There was one girl, an anaemic-looking creature with her face painted into a sharp foxiness, who was openly contemptuous of the audience. She may have been a disciple of Liz Brennan. The men took no notice. They sat through her act, twisting their heads about, and applauded politely at the end. She had no power to hurt them. No one really believed it.

It was then that Ponton understood what the striptease was all about and why the old men came. Monty had been right. It was a fantasy, a dream, but safer than dreams because they were unpredictable. There was no danger here. The women were as harmless as if they had been shut inside a transparent cage. They could insult the men, they could scream at them, but they could never do the one thing that would have shattered the dream. They could never come down from the stage and reach out and touch them, as Sylvia had once touched him. They offered a dream of sex which would never be realized, and so it could never be less than perfect. Inside this little box of shimmering lights it was fairyland, where everything is possible and nothing is true or false.

Suddenly Carla was on. It gave Ponton a shock. He had almost forgotten what he was there for. She was shuffling round the stage like a puppet on a string, jerking her bottom up and down mechanically and staring straight at him.

Carla finished her spot. She stood for a moment and received the few brief handclaps with a blank stare and a slight parting of the lips. As the curtain closed, she picked up her costume from the corner of the stage and padded back to the dressing room. It was her last spot and Thomas still wasn't there. Now she was really frightened. He was always there in time for her last spot. Sometimes he sat in one of the empty seats at the back making

148

faces at her, and sometimes he tried to come backstage and the other girls screamed and chased him out. He was always there. He knew she was afraid to go home alone. If he was with another woman she'd kill him. She got dressed as slowly as she could. One of the other girls asked her if she was all right. She didn't know what to say.

She gave him another ten minutes and then collected her things together and left the club without saying anything to anybody. She stood at the corner of Wardour Street and Old Compton Street, at the hub of the Soho wheel, and wondered what to do next. She was trying very hard not to panic. He might have forgotten the time and still be in his regular pub in Charing Cross Road. If she went there, she could keep to streets that were crowded and safe. It would be as quick to go straight back to the flat, but that meant empty streets where she could hear the sound of her own footsteps and dark doorways where the shadows flickered towards her. One day she'd move out of Soho altogether, perhaps even out of London, to somewhere quiet and green. She put her head down against the cold and pushed her way through the crowds along Old Compton Street. If he was on his way from the pub to meet her, this was the way he'd come.

As soon as she got inside the pub, she knew he wasn't there. He always sat in the same place. It was crowded with people jostling each other for space and she had to fight her way in. The seats along the front of the bar were full and she checked along the row of heads in case she'd missed him. She knew it was a waste of time but she was delaying the awful moment when she would have to go out into the street again and walk home alone. She spotted a barman she knew and elbowed her way across. She had to shout above the music and the conversation to make herself heard. No, he hadn't seen Thomas. He asked the others behind the bar. He'd been in at lunch-time but nobody had seen him since. She was getting frantic and it showed.

'Don't worry, love. He'll show up.'

'I need him now,' she said.

This was reported along the bar. A spotty white kid leaned across and grabbed her arm.

'Will I do?'

She turned and began to push her way out. Somebody shouted after her to have a drink.

Outside she kept to Charing Cross Road before cutting back

into Soho. It was a longer way round but there were more people here. Just before the corner with Oxford Street she turned left, away from the lights, with the dark mass of Soho Square in front of her. She just had to cross it and she was almost there. Her shadow kept slipping behind her as she walked under the street lights, then sliding along the wall to creep past her again. She began to walk more quickly. She had known from the moment she left the pub that she was being followed.

She'd bumped into him on her way out. He was on his way in. She was so agitated she hadn't even looked at him. She was just aware of a grey overcoat and a hand on her arm. She'd pushed past him and set off along Charing Cross Road. But the man hadn't gone into the pub. He'd turned and watched her for a moment and then started walking behind her. She didn't know how she knew all this because she hadn't looked back and she hadn't thought anything about it at the time. It had registered at the back of her mind, but it hadn't bothered her until she was halfway along the side road from Charing Cross into the square when she happened to look back and she saw him turn the corner behind her.

A car cruising slowly round Soho Square caught her in its headlights. She hesitated for a moment, then shot across in front of it, ducked down behind the parked cars and ran along the pavement beside the railings with her head down. She glanced into the park. A statue, which she was sure wasn't there in the daytime, seemed to be hovering just above the ground and watching her. When she got round to the other side of the semi-circle, she risked a quick look back. He was still there – or somebody was – coming past the railings at the top end of the square. She ran down Carlisle Street, across Dean Street, and zigzagged through the back roads towards her flat.

She got to the end of her street and looked along it. It seemed to be empty, but there was a bend in the middle so you could only see halfway. Her flat was just this side of the bend and the only street light was on the other side, so it was always dark and you never knew if there was anybody in the other half of the road until they were on top of you. She looked up at the window of her flat. If Thomas was there, the light would be on. It wasn't. She hurried on towards her door.

She opened the street door, took her shoes off for more speed, and ran up the stairs into the corridor. She reached out and flicked the light switch on. Nothing happened. She flicked it again and again. Nothing happened. There was no light. It was impossible. They'd just had it mended. She moved forward slowly in the darkness. She kicked something and sent it spinning down the corridor. It broke against one of the walls with a loud crack. She edged forward and trod on something. It was sharp and dug into her foot. There was another smaller piece sticking into the heel of her other foot. Whatever it was, it was all over the floor. She tucked her shoes under her arm and bent down and felt around. The floor was covered in bits of broken glass. It was a moment or two before she realized what it was. This time the light hadn't blown. It had been smashed.

She found the door. She'd already got her key out coming up the stairs. It took her ages to get it in the lock because she had her shoes under her arm, and she nearly dropped it. The key turned. When she was inside, she slammed the door and put the chain on and then went round the flat turning all the lights on. She stood in the doorway of the bedroom and had a good look round. She knew the danger was outside but she wasn't taking any chances. She crossed the room in one stride and threw the wardrobe door open. Then she did the same in the bathroom, pulling aside the shower curtain and having a look in the bath. She went round the flat again and checked that all the windows were locked.

When she was satisfied, she sat on the spare bed in the corner of the living room and examined her foot. There was a cut just under her big toe, oozing a drop of blood. She licked her finger and dabbed at it. Her heart was pumping and she had a pain in her chest. She looked around. Thomas's coat wasn't there. There was no sign that he'd been in all day. She sat on the bed and tried to calm herself down. There wasn't really anything to panic about. He could be anywhere. As for the man outside the pub, she didn't know for sure if he'd been following her and she couldn't be sure that he was the same man she'd seen in the square. That could have been anybody. She sat and took deep breaths and tried to pull herself together.

When she felt a bit better, she got up and took her coat off and put it away, hopping around on one foot. She lit the gas fire and went into the kitchen to look for a plaster. The kitchen was exactly as she'd left it that morning. There were no dirty dishes – a sure sign Thomas hadn't been there. She found a box of plasters in a cupboard and stuck one over her toe. Then she made herself a cup of coffee and came back and sat on the bed. She had just about managed to convince herself that she was being hysterical about nothing when she heard the floorboard squeak.

She knew which one it was. It was directly outside her door, the one that always squeaked when she stood there getting her key out. She gripped the side of the bed and called Thomas's name. She willed it to be him, but she didn't believe it for a minute.

She listened for the floorboard. There was no sound. She wondered if she could have imagined it. Very slowly and quietly she went over to the door and put her ear against it. She couldn't hear anything. She opened the door on the chain. It would only open a tiny crack with the chain on. Something passed in front of her and the floorboard squeaked again. She slammed the door and the chain fell out of its slot. She fumbled it into place and tugged on it to make sure it was in properly, then she backed away and stood in the middle of the floor, staring at the door with her fists clenched.

When Sylvia got to the street door that led up to Carla's flat, she had a good look round. There was nobody about but the light was on in Carla's window. She peered up the stairs. The little bit of light from the street reached about halfway up and the rest was in darkness. Her high heels clattered on the stairs. She got to the top. It was pitch black up here. She tried the light switch. It didn't work. She stood for a while at the top of the stairs and waited to see if her eyes got used to the dark. After a while she could see the wall beside her and she thought she could just make out the door of Carla's flat. She transferred her handbag to her left hand and felt her way along the wall until she got to the door. There was broken glass all over the floor. She knocked and heard a shuffling noise inside.

'Who is it?'

'It's me. Sylvia.' She thought she heard something move behind her and was about to turn round and look when the door opened an inch or two on the chain and Carla's nose appeared in the crack. 'Open the bloody door,' Sylvia said. 'It's freezing out here.'

'Is there anybody out there?'

'Yes, me. Open the door.'

The door closed and she heard the chain being taken off. The door began to open. At that moment Sylvia was pushed violently in the middle of her back, as if someone had fallen against her with his full weight. She fell forwards into the room. She tried to stop herself. She dropped her handbag and reached out for Carla who was standing in the middle of the floor. Carla stepped back and Sylvia landed in a heap in the corner and banged her head.

She must have blacked out for a minute. Her head was throbbing. She opened her eyes and looked across the room. Carla was sitting bolt upright on the edge of the bed, staring at the open door. Her eyes were wide open and rolled up so only the whites were showing, and her mouth was open in a scream.

Twenty-two

Ponton couldn't believe he'd lost her. One minute she was there and the next she'd completely vanished. She'd looked round a couple of times and he was afraid she might have spotted him so he'd dropped back a bit, and then she was gone. He stood and looked around him. He wasn't sure where he was, but he knew that Oxford Street was somewhere off to his right. There were streets going in all directions, all rather dark and creepy and none giving any indication that Carla might be lurking at the end of it. He picked a street at random and wandered down it. There was a low, blank wall on one side. On the other side were doorways, all dark. What was he expecting? Carla hanging out of a window and whistling at him? By now she was safely indoors somewhere. It had been a ridiculous idea anyway.

He had nowhere else to go so he picked another street and set off along it, looking up at the windows. What was he supposed to do now? Start knocking on doors? It was a dark, narrow street with a bend in the middle so he couldn't see how long it was. He walked as far as the bend and stood under a street light. The other half was the same as the first. More doorways, more windows. This was hopeless. He turned and walked back the way he had come. He was almost at the corner when he heard the scream.

Sylvia was not so much frightened as fascinated by the spectacle that was crossing the room towards her. Actually, he didn't seem to be taking any notice of her. He was staring at Carla, who was sitting on the bed staring back at him. Sylvia only had to look at her to know she was useless. She was sitting right on the edge with her shoulders hunched up and her fingers dug into the mattress.

She had screamed once and her mouth was still open, but she didn't seem able to move.

Sylvia wondered if she could get past him. He didn't seem to be interested in her, or even aware that she was there. She could probably have got to the open door and out to find help, but by the time she found anybody Carla would be dead. Sylvia had no doubt that he intended to kill her. She could hardly recognize him. She had never seen a face so twisted and distorted.

He was trying to say something but the words wouldn't come out. He crossed the room towards Carla with his arms out in front of him, walking stiff-legged like a monster in a film and spluttering, trying to get the words out. He never took his eyes off Carla's face. Sylvia knew it was all up to her. She looked round for her handbag. She always kept it well stocked and heavy enough to floor an elephant. It had fallen too far away, in the other corner by the bed. That only left her with one alternative. Right, she thought, here goes. She'd never been afraid of him before.

She stood up and screamed as loud as she could. Slowly he took his eyes off Carla, turned, and started towards her. When she was looking him straight in the face, she didn't know if she'd be able to do it. Then she remembered Liz. This was the last thing she'd ever seen.

When he was just close enough to touch her, she hit him with all her strength. It was a long swinging uppercut that went between his arms and caught him on the side of the jaw. Judging by the pain in her fingers, it was a good one. He tottered for a moment with his arms flailing like a tightrope walker losing balance, and fell backwards on the floor. Sylvia came down on top of him, letting herself drop dead-weight on his chest and stomach. She grabbed his hair at the sides where it was thickest and started banging his head on the floor. She went on until he had stopped struggling. When she looked up, Ponton was standing in the doorway.

'Are you all right?' he said.

She stared at him. It struck her as the silliest question she'd ever heard and she nearly started laughing. She couldn't understand what he was doing there. She wondered if he was really there at all or if she was imagining him. She looked down at the body she was sitting on. It was still breathing but there was no other sign of life. She thought it was safer to stay on top of him for a while.

'You know who it is, don't you?'

155

'Yes,' Ponton said. 'It would appear to be Eric.'

Ponton phoned Inspector Wright and everything bar the fire brigade arrived shortly after. There were hordes of police and an ambulance crew. He had apparently given the impression over the phone that a small massacre had taken place. The police scraped Eric up off the floor and led him away. He offered no resistance. Carla was taken away by two nice men in white coats, with a policeman's jacket over her shoulders, gibbering quietly to herself. Sylvia complained of a headache.

'And I've broken my fingers.'

One of the ambulance men had a look at her hand and declared her good for another fifteen rounds.

'Cheeky sod,' she said.

Ponton and Sylvia were taken out to the police cars, which were parked in Dean Street. A small crowd had formed. Ponton tried to bury his head in his coat and was no doubt assumed by the onlookers to be the criminal party. Sylvia looked like a film star arriving at a premiere. Carla had been put in the ambulance and was driven away. Ponton never saw her again. Eric was in the car behind. Ponton caught a glimpse of him sitting on the back seat between two policemen, looking dazed. One of the policemen was examining his jaw with a look of professional curiosity. They were driven quickly out of Soho and across Piccadilly Circus with the sirens blaring. Ponton looked round to check that Eric's car was behind them in the swirl of traffic.

When the convoy arrived at the police station, there were men in uniform running in all directions. Eric was bundled out of the car and disappeared upstairs in a rugby scrum of policemen. Ponton and Sylvia were left standing by the front door wondering what they were supposed to be doing, and Ponton was looking for a place to hide. There was one small group of people who had not been involved in the pandemonium caused by Eric's arrival. At the centre of this group stood a familiar figure in tweeds, accompanied by an elderly gentleman who was cowering behind her. Mrs Maitland was haranguing the desk sergeant and a couple of young constables who, from what Ponton could hear, had had the temerity to arrest her for causing an obstruction. Ponton tried to make himself invisible, to no avail. She spotted him.

'And what is going on here?' she demanded, marching across to where Ponton was standing. He didn't feel like telling her. She transferred her attention to Sylvia and the expression on her face indicated that she had identified Sylvia's occupation, or at least narrowed it down to one of two. But Sylvia was not looking at Mrs Maitland. She was looking at the little ferret face who had remained by the desk and was trying very hard not to be noticed.

'Hello,' she said, giving him a wave, 'haven't seen you for a while.'

Mr Maitland turned towards her with a face like death.

'Donald,' his wife said, in a voice of thunder, as he came shuffling over to join them, 'do you know this person?'

Mr Maitland was speechless. He had turned an awful colour. He gave Sylvia a look of utter panic. She got her bearings.

'Oh,' she said, digging Ponton in the ribs, 'I'm terribly sorry. I seem to have made a mistake. I'm always doing that. I thought I knew your husband from somewhere.'

'That,' said Mrs Maitland, 'is exceedingly unlikely. Donald, come.'

She returned to her argument with the constables. Mr Maitland trotted behind her, but he looked back at Sylvia with an expression of gratitude beyond words.

Ponton was looking puzzled.

'Lemon sweets,' Sylvia hissed in his ear, digging him in the ribs again and nodding towards the departing Donald. Ponton gave her a disapproving look. 'Well,' she said, 'poor old devil. I always said he was harmless. And the police won't be interested in him now it's all over, will they?' She looked anxiously at Ponton. 'It is over, isn't it?'

'I don't know,' he said.

The next few hours were a nightmare. For months after, Ponton would wake up in the early hours of the morning with visions of the inspector's glasses flashing at him and the hairy finger wagging.

He was taken to a room where he made a statement. When he read it through, it made no sense at all. He made it again. Sylvia was in the next room doing the same. When he was satisfied, he waited for it to be typed, signed it, and then hung around for ages, wandering up and down corridors and reading notice-boards, while attempts were made upstairs to get a coherent statement out of Eric. Apparently it was proving difficult, not least because of his battered condition and his fears that Sylvia might be let loose on him again. At one point, when he was sick of the sight of the police station, Ponton walked down to Piccadilly Circus, had a look around, and came back via Regent Street. It was after midnight and freezing cold, cold enough for snow, but the streets were still full of people. He couldn't imagine what they were all doing.

Eventually he was summoned back to Inspector Wright's office. He found the inspector sitting behind his desk with a sheet of paper, similar to the one which Ponton had signed, clutched in a hairy paw. He waved the paper in the direction of a chair and Ponton sat down. The inspector was looking even hairier than usual. He must have missed his second or third shave of the day because the stubble was beginning to sprout along the side of his face and down his neck. It seemed to start under his eyes. He looked like a chimpanzee with the delicate, rimless glasses perched absurdly on the bridge of its nose.

'Your nephew,' he said, putting the sheet of paper down on his desk, 'has been rather naughty.'

'So it would appear,' Ponton said.

'And your Mr Redgrove ...' the voice went on in the same flat tone but there was a little dramatic pause, ' ... has been rather naughty too.'

'Yes, I suppose he has.' Ponton was taken aback. He had not expected this.

'Withholding evidence,' the inspector said in a booming voice. The finger wagged. 'You knew about that?'

'Yes, I'm afraid I did.'

'It does help, you know,' the inspector said, in a voice of infinite sadness, 'if people tell us things.'

'I'm sure it does. I'm sorry.'

'Well,' he said, 'I don't suppose it's worth going into that now.' He pushed the sheet of paper across the desk. 'You'd better read that. We might need your support.'

'Why?'

The inspector took his glasses off and cleaned them with a large handkerchief. His eyes were red. He looked a very tired chimpanzee.

'We've cautioned him,' he said slowly, stressing each syllable, 'and we've charged him. And I can't honestly say I think he understood a word of either.' He nodded at the statement in Ponton's hand. 'We've got it down on paper, but I don't know

158

whether he's got much idea what he's said. And it's anybody's guess what he'll say next time. I'm not at all sure he'll be fit to plead.'

'So there won't be a trial?'

'I doubt it.' He leaned back in his chair and looked up at the ceiling. 'There is also the consideration that apart from that piece of paper, and tonight's little incident, we don't have a shred of evidence against him.'

'I see,' Ponton said. 'So a plea of insanity might be in order?'

'It would be quite wrong for me to advise you,' the inspector leaned across the desk and his eyes disappeared behind the glasses, 'but if someone were to enter such a plea on his behalf, I think it would be looked upon quite favourably.'

Ponton nodded, got a pipe going, and read through Eric's statement slowly. It was garbled but intelligible. He imagined it must have needed quite a bit of polishing to be as clear as it was. There was a great deal of ranting and raving, but the gist of it was that Eric had killed Liz Brennan for reasons which made a sort of half-sense if you knew Eric, and that he had gone after Carla out of revenge because she had killed Vicky in a fight. Ponton finished reading and pushed the paper back across the desk. It was what he had expected.

'Thank you,' he said.

'Well, what do you think?'

'I believe the first part but I do not believe the second.'

'No, sir,' the inspector said, 'neither do we.'

Ah yes, Ponton thought, but that does not necessarily mean that we believe the same thing.

Twenty-three

It was some time in the early hours of the morning when the police finished with them, and Ponton and Sylvia walked back to her flat together. She had offered to put him up on the sofa. He had said no. She had asked him where he was going to sleep. He said he didn't know but he would find somewhere. She told him not to be stupid, slipped her arm through his, and they set off back into Soho. The streets, at last, were deserted. The shops and clubs were closed, with corrugated sheets pulled down over the doorways and padlocked, and the lights switched off. It could have been any night in the centre of any town in England. They walked arm in arm without speaking.

As they turned out of Shaftesbury Avenue into Soho, she had stopped and stood for a moment with her head on his shoulder and her fingers digging into his wrist. He waited without responding, without looking at her, until she was ready to go on. She now had both arms twisted through his, and she was leaning on him and holding his hand as she walked. The sleeve of her coat was rubbing against his hand. It was the same coat she had worn that night in his rooms in Highgate. It was supposed to be fur but it was some kind of fake. It looked as if it would have been smooth and silky, but it was rough and stubbly to the touch. He found the coat offensive, like an artificial Christmas tree. He found Sylvia offensive. He couldn't understand how he'd ever liked her, how he'd managed to get some silly, schoolboyish thrill out of knowing this woman who was the antithesis of everything he should have found attractive. Probably that was the reason. He had enjoyed acting against type. Whatever would his colleagues have said? Boring old Tony, the old maid of the faculty, and his friend the striptease dancer.

Halfway along Greek Street, she turned into a doorway. She disengaged her arms and led the way up the stairs. It was the same arrangement as Carla's – a staircase, a dark corridor with peeling wallpaper and a door into a tiny flat. They took their coats off and got the fire going.

'Do you think we could have something to eat?' Ponton said. 'I don't seem to have had any dinner.' He was more tired than hungry. He'd got past the hungry stage hours ago. It had been a long day and all he wanted to do was sleep, but he knew he couldn't yet. The food might wake him up.

'Sandwiches all right?' she said.

'Fine.'

Sylvia went into the bedroom to get changed. She didn't even bother closing the door. She stood behind it and tossed her clothes across the open doorway on to the bed, and then emerged in a dressing gown, quite modest, and went into the kitchen. The room had begun to warm up and Ponton took his jacket off and settled himself in an armchair.

The flat was tiny and crammed with furniture and ornaments in the most appalling taste he had ever come across. The walls were covered in posters of what he took to be pop musicians. The most dominant one, almost life-size, featured a young man with long hair and an expression of acute agony, holding an electric guitar jammed between his legs like a grotesque phallus. Ranged immediately below it on a shelf was a row of indescribably twee model animals, like a child's toy zoo. There was only one book in the room, lying on the floor. It had something red and sticky on the cover, and Ponton picked it up by one corner like somebody holding a dead rat by the tail. It was a detective story. An eye-shadow brush fell out.

Sylvia returned with a large plate of bacon sandwiches and coffee on a tray. She put the tray on the floor while she moved a little table into the space between the two armchairs, then put the tray on the table, making exaggerated efforts to keep the dressing gown closed across her breasts.

'Is that all right? I thought you'd prefer coffee.'

'Yes,' he said. 'Lovely.'

Ponton drank his coffee and Sylvia made herself comfortable in the other armchair and started on the sandwiches. When they had finished eating, Ponton lit a pipe. Sylvia had found a packet of cigarettes at the back of a drawer and was turning it over and over between her fingers.

'Did you get to see Eric?' she said.

'No, I read his statement.'

'He killed Liz.' Ponton wasn't sure whether this was meant as a question or not.

'Yes,' he said, 'I don't think there's any doubt about that. He was infatuated with her and she somehow betrayed him, or he thought she had. And by then he'd transferred his obsession to Vicky. When she died, he went berserk. He got it into his head that Carla had killed her, and he went after her for revenge.'

'Oh. That's that, then.'

'Why do you think he was so sure it was Carla?' Ponton said, as if he were enquiring disinterestedly, just for information.

'That's easy.' Sylvia wasn't looking at him. She had finally taken a cigarette out of the packet and lit it, and she was watching the smoke drift up to the ceiling. 'They had a fight. Everybody knew about it. Carla wanted the name and Vicky wouldn't give it to her.'

'Yes, Mr X again.' His pipe had gone out and he took some time to get it going. He had to be careful with this bit. He was still determined to keep David out of it. 'But you see the problem ...' He applied one final match to the pipe... 'Carla's money was nothing to do with him. Mr X, whoever he was, paid some money to Liz and Vicky once, and that, I believe, was the end of his part in the story. I don't suppose we shall ever know who he was. But I happen to know where Carla got that money. It was because of something she knew about Vicky, something she saw. The stuff about Mr X was just a story, to cover up where the money was really coming from. So you see the problem?'

'No.' She still wouldn't look at him.

'There never was a fight. Well, not with Carla, anyway.'

'Oh.'

'I imagine the police will draw the conclusion that Eric committed both murders. They'd have a job proving it but they may not have to. But there are other possibilities. You see, I find myself asking who else was there, who else was in Vicky's flat that night?'

Sylvia said nothing. Ponton took a while to achieve a satisfactory symmetry among the objects on the little table between their chairs. Then he looked at her, and waited.

'Did you have anybody in mind?' she said.

'Yes.'

She finished her cigarette, fumbled open the packet, took another one out and then put it back again. She crossed her legs and sat for a while fingering the hem of her dressing gown.

'It was an accident,' she said. 'I'm sure it was.'

There was a long pause. Ponton puffed on his pipe and waited. He had foreseen this moment hours ago. He was not in a hurry.

'I went round to see her,' she said, 'like I told you, to find out if she'd see you. She was horrible. Said she hated Eric, hated me, hated everybody. You don't know what she could be like. Anyway, I was expecting all that. I'd hēard it all before. Then she started talking about Liz. How she despised her. How Liz was stupid, almost as stupid as me. How she was past it. Couldn't get a man if she wanted one.' Ponton was going to offer her a handkerchief but she fished one out of her pocket and blew her nose. 'You know, Liz was the only friend she had. Got her into the clubs, looked after her, talked to her when nobody else would. She was one of the best, Liz. One of the best.' Sylvia was beginning to cry. She had a rest and started again. 'I hit her. Not hard. It was meant to be a slap across the face. I suppose it was a punch. I hadn't realized how light she was. She just went straight over backwards. Hit her head on the sink. I could tell she was dead.'

'Then you picked the phone up?'

Sylvia leaned forward in her chair.

'I was going to call the police. Really I was. Then I started thinking so I put it down again.'

'You didn't put it back properly. It must have been off the hook all night. Go on.'

'Well, then it hit me. There was a murderer loose. I swear to God I didn't know it was Eric. But somebody had killed Liz. Somebody had done one murder and he was going to get caught for it sooner or later. So why not get caught for two? Nobody'd believe him if they were done the same way. He wouldn't be any worse off and I'd be a hell of a lot better off. He had it coming and I didn't. He was a cold-blooded murderer and I was somebody who didn't know my own strength. So why shouldn't he get the blame for both? That's fair, isn't it?'

This was stated with such obvious conviction that Ponton was rather taken aback. He didn't feel like arguing.

'Go on.'

'So I set it up to look like Liz's murder.' Sylvia's whole mood had changed. She was getting excited with her story, her triumph, twisting the end of the handkerchief round her fingers. 'I had a hammock the same as Vicky's. I got it once when I was going to copy her act. Never used it. I think I told you.'

'Yes,' Ponton said. 'I remembered eventually.'

'Well, I came home and got it and took it back. Then I took her clothes off and stuck the hammock round her neck. Next morning I got to Monty's early, found Vicky's hammock, shoved it in a paper bag and walked out with it. Nobody was looking for it then. By the time the police came, it was back here in the wardrobe. Easy.'

She lit another cigarette and re-crossed her legs. The dressing gown had fallen open at her breasts and legs, and she lounged back in the armchair with her hand beside her head, palm open, the cigarette lodged between two fingers. She looked completely relaxed, as if she was waiting for congratulations.

'There's one thing I don't understand,' Ponton said. 'Why didn't you let me go back to Southampton that day? Why did you insist that we discuss the murders?'

'I wanted to be sure I'd covered my tracks. If you hadn't spotted anything, I reckoned I was safe. I couldn't very well ask the police how I was doing, could I?'

'I see,' he said. 'Thank you. That explains a number of things.' He was relieved. His last remaining doubt about Sylvia had been removed.

'Like what?' she said belligerently.

'It doesn't matter.'

'I want to know what it explains.'

'You wanted to find out whether I suspected you. That was very clever of you. I understand.'

'Don't understand so bloody fast.'

'It really doesn't matter.'

'Look,' she said, 'what I did in your room that night. I wasn't pretending. That was nothing to do with it. I'd already found out what I wanted to know. What do you think I am?' She stubbed her cigarette out and pulled her dressing gown straight. Ponton had almost disappeared in a cloud of tobacco smoke. 'You're going to turn me in,' she said, 'aren't you? You're going to tell the police.'

'Yes, I have to.'

'Why? Because you hate me?'

'No.'

164

'Why?'

'You're not going to understand.'

'Try me. I know I'm thick but try.'

'Because this is real. This is the real world. It's not the clubs where you can believe anything you like. Your killing Vicky was a real action with consequences that have to be faced. Do you understand?'

'No. I think you just want to see me punished.'

Ponton gave up.

'You have no moral sense whatsoever.'

'Yes I have,' she said. 'I know what's right and wrong. I know killing Vicky was wrong even if she was a cow. But it was an accident. Sending me to prison, or whatever they do to me, that isn't going to do any good. It's not going to bring her back. It's just going to ruin my life. That's not good. There's nothing good about that. You don't know what good is. You think being good is the same as being miserable.'

'That's absurd.'

'Is it? Just because you're lonely and miserable you want everybody to be lonely and miserable. You want me punished so you can believe in good and bad. You're good and I'm bad. The real reason you want me punished isn't anything to do with Vicky. It's because you fancy me. It's because I nearly got you in bed. You shut yourself up with a wall round you so nobody can get in and I got through. I frightened the life out of you. That's what you can't forgive me for. You're the great brainbox and I'm thick and I undress for a living and you wanted me. Now I'm going to be locked away so you can pretend it never happened.'

'You're talking nonsense,' he said. 'You're tired. We're both tired. I'm not going to discuss it any more tonight.' He stood up and went over to the window and looked out at a blank wall.

'Bugger tired,' she said. 'What are you doing up here anyway? You didn't come up to see me. What were you doing hanging around outside Carla's?'

He stood looking out of the window and said nothing. She was quiet for a while. Then he heard the rustle of her dressing gown as she got up and came over and stood behind him. When she spoke, it was much more calmly and slowly, as if she was trying to work things out.

'That time you phoned me,' she said, 'about Carla. You already knew about the money. You knew it had happened twice. You knew she was blackmailing somebody. Didn't you?'

'Yes,' he said. When she started thinking, you could hear the wheels turning.

'How?'

'He was a friend of mine.' He didn't care what he told her now. It was the one thing he had been trying to keep from her all along, and it no longer mattered. Tell her everything and let her make what she likes out of it. He just wanted her to shut up and go away so he could go to bed and sleep. He was desperately tired.

'Who was a friend of yours?'

'He had an affair with Vicky,' Ponton said very slowly. 'He lied to the police. Carla found out about it.'

'Your friend?'

'YES!' He had turned round and screamed at her. She was standing an inch away with her dressing gown hanging off and her stupid face gawping at him, streaked with make-up.

'So that's it.' Her eyes opened wide. 'Did you go to the police about this friend of yours?'

'No.'

'I bet you didn't.' Her mind was working now as it had never worked before. He could hear it. 'You want it all tidied up. You want Eric in prison and me in prison and the whole business over and done with and nobody asking any more questions. You don't want the police asking questions about your friend. That's it.'

'No,' he said, 'you stupid bitch, that is not it. They already know about him.'

'That's what you say. You want me out of the way and nobody asking any questions.' She stood in front of him with her hands on her hips. 'What is he,' she said, 'your bloody boyfriend?' and she burst out laughing.

Then Ponton hit her. All the anger and the pain welled up inside him and he lashed out. It had been uncontrollable. He was appalled. He had never hit anyone before in his life. Sylvia rode the blow like a boxer.

Twenty-four

In the weeks which followed these events, something took effect which Ponton called the law of epistemological inertia. And what, Sylvia had asked him, was that when it was at home? It was Sunday morning and she was lying in bed in the house in Southampton. She was on one of her weekend visits.

Ponton lit his post-breakfast pipe and explained. It was, he said, a law which operates when there is a particularly difficult problem which requires urgent solution and when the existence of that problem is an embarrassment to a number of important people. The law states that as soon as a solution offers itself which roughly fits the facts and tidies up the loose ends, it becomes irresistibly convincing and objections to it become invisible.

Sylvia gave her pillows a thorough pummelling, sat up and thought about this for a while.

'You mean they've got Eric locked up and that's the end of it.'

'Exactly.'

'Good,' she said. She turned over and gave every appearance of going back to sleep. It was amazing how long she could lie in bed in the morning.

She was staying over a second night as they were invited round to the Redgroves for dinner that evening. David and Janet were holding a belated celebration of their latest reconciliation. Sylvia had been a nine-days wonder among Ponton's small circle of friends at the university. He had been very apprehensive about showing her off at first, but she was not the sort of person who could be kept locked up in the house. After the initial shock, everybody had been very nice and they seemed genuinely pleased that he was no longer on his own. Her appearance had also put paid to a number of people's pet theories about Ponton's sexual preferences. Janet, in particular, had received her with wide-eyed amazement, but they now got on very well. David was charming but correct. Sylvia was not exactly his type. Ponton didn't know what people said about her in private, of course, but neither was he unduly bothered. Presumably they accepted that he was old enough and ugly enough to know what he was doing.

As Inspector Wright had predicted, Eric was found unfit to plead. This was helpful since there was no direct evidence to convict him of anything – beyond his confession, which was unreliable and simply served to complicate matters. Carla had vigorously denied ever laying a finger on Vicky, and the police believed her.

Under the provisions of the Criminal Procedure (Insanity) Act 1964, Eric was sent to an institution which Sylvia called the funny farm, with a tacit agreement all round that his stay was to be an indefinite one. This might have caused a bit of bother with the family since an appeal against the order was possible, but the authorities were gratified when Mr Ponton, the uncle, expressed his immediate and total approval of the plan. Officially the murders of Elizabeth Brennan and Victoria Tate remain on the records of the Metropolitan Police as crimes for which no conviction was ever obtained. Unofficially, if anyone should enquire into them, he will be given a nod and a wink and an assurance that they were in fact solved and that the culprit is now in a place where he can do no further harm.

Eric proved to be a model prisoner, or patient, or whatever he was, though he had given some cause for concern at first. On some days he confessed to Liz's murder. On other days he confessed to murdering both Liz and Vicky. Sometimes he claimed he had murdered Liz but Carla had murdered Vicky. And sometimes he denied everything. Eventually he stopped talking about it, to everyone's great relief, and began to concentrate on his rehabilitation. He had discovered a previously unsuspected talent for taking motor-bicycles to pieces and putting them together again. He had also discovered God.

The police had established to their own satisfaction that it would have been physically possible for him to travel from Southampton at dead of night, murder Vicky, and return to his bed without anyone having noticed. Again, his uncle had been obliging enough to agree that this was entirely feasible. His visit to Vicky's flat the following morning, previously a bit of a puzzle, was now explained. It was a classic case of the criminal returning to the scene of the crime, to check that he had not been careless, or to gloat over his victim, or whatever happened to be in his head at the time.

At this point Ponton's law had come into effect. Any need to prove that this was what he had really done was avoided by the fact of his never standing trial, and the need to take account of his varying confessions was avoided by his having been declared raving mad by all competent authorities. The newspapers, who might have noticed that the Striptease Murders had not been entirely resolved, were more interested in what was becoming known as the winter of discontent and in the antics of an increasingly beleaguered government. On January the 10th, the Prime Minister had arrived back from the Caribbean and announced that there was no crisis. The press had licked its lips and the nation braced itself for trouble.

One morning in March, Ponton was making one of his periodic visits to Eric. He tried to go every month and he was usually accompanied by his sister, but she had not been feeling well for a number of days and so he had come on his own. He was relieved about this. The woman was an absolute pest. She insisted on believing that Eric was innocent of everything and had merely fallen into bad company.

Ponton and Eric sat together in a room very like the one in the police station where they had had their conversation after Vicky's death, except that the furniture was a bit more comfortable and the door had a little window with a panel that slid across, presumably so that somebody could have a look in from time to time and make sure they weren't murdering each other.

Ponton had been assured that Eric was making remarkable progress, and he had to admit that he was looking much better than on previous occasions. He was wearing a bright, checkered shirt and quite a respectable pair of jeans. He'd even had a haircut, which emphasized how thin he was getting on top. He looked like a monk having the day off. His hands were filthy and there was half an inch of grease under his fingernails, but this was acceptable in view of his new-found talents. He was perfectly calm and reasonable, as he had been on the last couple of visits, but

Ponton still found him a bit scary. He sat too close, smiled all the time, and never took his eyes off Ponton's face. The more he smiled, the more reasonable he was, the more Ponton found himself looking round the room for a blunt instrument in case he should need to protect himself by cracking Eric over the head with it.

When Ponton had begun making his visits, he had been warned never to discuss the murders. It now appeared that Eric could be allowed and even encouraged to discuss them, as he was able to do so sensibly and without getting upset or over-exciting himself. Everyone was very pleased with him and Eric was properly proud of his achievement.

After he had asked the usual questions about Eric's health, and listened to a full account of the condition of the motor-bike which Eric was working on, Ponton asked him rather hesitantly if he remembered Liz Brennan.

'Oh yes,' he said. His eyes glittered at the opportunity to display his prowess, and he leaned forward across the table until their noses almost touched.

'What do you remember?' Ponton said.

'I was very silly about her.'

'In what way?'

'I thought she was the one. I thought she was perfect. But she wasn't. It was Vicky who was perfect.'

'Yes,' Ponton said.

'Liz was bad. Very bad. That night at the party, she told everybody, you know.' Eric smiled to show how sensible he was being. 'She said it was all a game. She was just play-acting. She told everybody, with me sitting there. And they all laughed. She made a fool of me. That was very bad of her.' He smiled.

'Yes,' Ponton said, 'very bad.'

'And Carla. What she did. She killed Vicky. That was very bad too.' He smiled again.

'Yes.' Ponton smiled. It was infectious.

'But I've forgiven her, you know. And Liz.' Eric smiled his forgiveness. He moved even closer, shuffling his elbows across the table and fixing his gaze on Ponton. 'It took a long time. But I can forgive them now because I know I've been forgiven. He told me I'd been forgiven.'

'Who told you?' Ponton was afraid he already knew the answer.

'God.'

170